MW01242461

# Chained

# Chained

Alyson Jensen

HUMBLE SHACK, LLC.

Copyright © 2021 by Humble Shack, LLC.

All rights reserved. This book or any portion thereof may not be reproduced or used in any manner whatsoever without the express written permission of the publisher except for the use of brief quotations in a book review.

Printed in the United States of America.

Humble Shack, LLC.
5150A Albert Evans Rd. S.
Wilmer, AL, 36587

HumbleShack.net

Map by Alyson Jensen and Esther Jensen. ©

*To Jesus Christ,*
*For His unfailing love, His beckoning call*
*and His acceptance of all who call on Him*
*to be saved.*

*To Mom and Dad,*
*Who have dutifully and lovingly taught me*
*about the Lord and His salvation plan.*

Any resemblance in this book to any person, place, or thing – living or dead – just might be on purpose.

# The Fallen Lands
## Chahcan

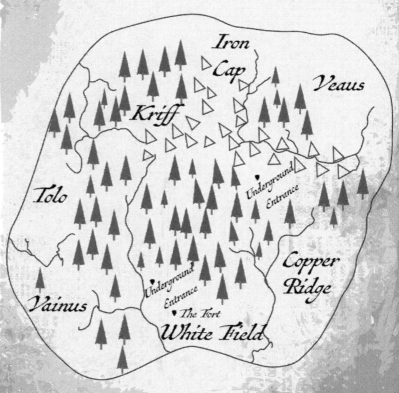

Iron Cap

Veaus

Kriff

Tolo

Underground Entrance

Underground Entrance

Copper Ridge

Vainus

The Fort

White Field

Design by Alyson and Esther Jensen. ©

# Prologue

Golden rays from the first moments of sunset lent their radiance to the glades of Chahcan's dense forestry while two men quietly convened in one of the many staunch tents.

"Did you make contact with him?" one man asked. The other shook his head.

"He just slipped past us, Commander," was the verbal reply. The commander slapped his right hand against his leg.

"That's the third time," he exclaimed, holding up the appropriate number of fingers. "How does the boy manage it?"

"He's recluse, for one thing," the second man added. "We'd have to break into his house just to get a word with him. Otherwise, draw attention in another uncivil manner."

"And you're sure that you've got the right kid?" the commander queried.

"I wouldn't hound him to the ends of the Fallen Lands if I wasn't sure," the second man replied with a grin.

"Don't tease, Colin," the commander warned.

"Look, Ren confirmed it. You were there yourself when he said so. Why the uncertainty now?" Colin asked. The commander frowned.

"Well, let's just say it certainly doesn't seem like the time has come. I have thought before, and I must say now, perhaps it is the wrong time. Maybe the Lord does not mean…"

"No, Commander," Colin interjected. "The Lord said 'now.' We have been waiting our whole lives for this prophecy's fulfillment. Are we going to stall yet again after three failures? At least, give it one attempt for every year we have waited. Twenty-five."

"Twenty-six," the commander corrected.

"Forgive me. That's all the better for my cause," Colin joyfully agreed. The commander gave a small chuckle and nodded slowly.

"You know that I dream of this prophecy's fulfillment as others. I am willing, Colin."

"Yes, but it seems the promised one isn't," Colin added.

"First comes the prophecy's fulfillment, then the Pure Line will take his rightful position," the commander calmly reminded his friend. "What we need is a new angle. Or a new agent. Someone who can make contact without arousing outside suspicion."

"The Lord knows we can't have the Ruling Heads after us," Colin laughed.

Chahcan was a country of the strangest ruling system. Chahcan had had its kings and queens but was past that time. It had not one leading figure, but several – the richest, most influential men of the country. Even Chahcan's militia was under their powerful influence.

The commander and his group had been disfavored for many years, resulting in the desire of their death.

"Come now, speak seriously," the commander presently resumed. "Who do you know among us who could be enlisted into such a service?"

"Try the rich lass," Colin suggested, without hesitation. "I know she already has an acquaintance with someone of close proximity to the boy. Give her the message and let her have a go." With a slight shrug, the commander stepped outside to pace in front of the tent's entrance. His friend's idea had great credibility. The girl had plenty of exposure in Chahcan, so her actions would go unnoticed. Her parents would ensure her safety. Also, he knew that she could be entrusted with a secret, no matter how small or monumental. There was just one matter that unsettled him.

"What about supplies?" the commander finally asked, turning back to face Colin. "She's been the most successful in delivering the quota."

"I'll find a way to solve that personally if you give her a whirl," Colin promised heartily.

"All right. I trust you," the commander smiled. "Just don't get crazy."

"Since when was I crazy?" Colin wondered. The commander smirked and gave his friend a knowing look.

"Here's the deal: don't get killed and don't get anyone else killed," he clarified, seating himself at a low rock which made his table.

"I shall strive not to suffer that consequence," Colin replied with a twinkle in his blue eyes. "As to anything of less seriousness, I will try not to venture beyond a joke." The commander held his quill above a fresh sheet of paper, meanwhile turning to his friend with a stoic expression.

"Thank you," he said simply. "You may go now. I'll write the girl."

Colin nodded. "I'll send someone by to deliver it," he decided. The commander paused in the act of writing and looked up once more.

"What did you say the kid's name was?"

"Adrian Falkner."

# CHAPTER ONE

## Lost Inside Myself

The wind swept up sand, creating a small whirlwind that slapped into me and then dissipated every few minutes. The sultry sting added to the blistering heat of August. I suspected that the region of Copper Ridge was unvisited by anyone of importance based solely on its weather. Walking down the primary, cobblestone road, I passed the homes of the local merchants and shop owners.

Further along, the stores themselves were located. Several were open-air, with no real building, just a space in which that person did their practice. The blacksmith's place was always open and for an excellent reason, too. The livery stable was across the street, but I could still catch a whiff of horse manure. I practically jogged up the steps and into the Market, ready to get in, do business, and get out.

The Market was the main trading center in all of Copper Ridge. If one thought that the building outside was terrible with its rusted metal roof and simple wood building construction, then they weren't ready to see the inside. An abundance of wooden shelves covered the barren walls holding canned food, sacks of flour, and tins of sugar. Several barrels lined a pathway to the small counter with a clunky register. The large window in the front of the structure was opened, letting in the hot air.

"Whatcha need this time, Adrian?" the shop owner asked as I stepped through the door. I handed him a list of items my mother had left for me; it was full of things she needed. He got right to work.

"Ah, folks real busy?" he asked, pulling cans off a shelf. I shrugged and looked around the shop once more. I didn't know what my parents were doing, but I assumed they were busy. He didn't press for more information.

"Okay, corn, beans, bread," he read the list aloud as he stacked the items on the short counter. "How do you expect to carry all these things here?" I barely heard him. I was looking out the open window, watching people run past the shop front. I frowned and watched as more people ran and screamed.

"Did ya hear me?" the owner asked, raising his voice. As quickly as they had come, all the people disappeared off the streets. I could still hear yells not too far away. I turned back to the manager.

"I can manage," I told him. He shrugged and continued to slide the needed things across the counter toward me. My eyes were on the scene outside, where a group of men carrying shovels and buckets jogged past. That didn't look right, so I stepped out onto the street for a better view. From there, I could see the house in the distance that was on fire. I stepped further into the street.

"Hey, Adrian, your food?" the shop owner called. I waved him off.

"I'll be back," I said, then took off running for the scene. As I got closer, the structure of the house and the figures of more and more people became clearer. The men of the town stood their distance from the house, buckets at the ready, but not moving to fight the fire. The red-orange flames covered every part of the house, and licked the air above as smoke formed dark clouds in the sky. As I was running, the roof collapsed, spraying sparks at the crowd. It wasn't until I got there that I realized the good-sized group of men who stood, cloaked in black, swords and bows raised, between our men and the burning house. I suddenly spotted Alex Ziegler, my best friend, and at the same time, he saw me. He ran over.

"Tyrrohns," Alex muttered. I nodded. The term made my spine tingle. Groups like these often stirred up trouble in Chahcan's capital. Copper Ridge had merely taken the ripple effects of tyrrohn destruction and rise to power. The tyrrohns' apparent leader finished fueling the fire and turned to the gathered crowd.

"There is more for you to lose," he said in a loud voice. "My master is lord over all of you; he controls your next loss. Speak! Tell me where the fighters hide." Alex looked to me as if to ask if I knew. I shrugged, and we exchanged confused looks.

"What happens to us if we don't know what your master wants?" a man shouted from the crowd.

"Forgotten, huh?" The leader lit another torch and threw it into the nearest house. People screamed and ran from the building. "Remember now?" No one answered. "My master is not a patient man. He will not stand your silence," the man shouted. His eyes stared hard at each man in turn. No one dared to offer another answer. They must not have known any more about these fighters than I did.

The tyrrohn leader motioned to one of his men. "Burn a few more and kill anyone who threatens you," he ordered. I stared at the strange group of men as they went to perform the task. There was something wrong with their appearance, other than their cloaks and weapons. They seemed to be floating above the ground instead of walking on it. I moved forward, trying to get a closer look. Alex grabbed my arm.

"Are you crazy? He just threatened to kill anyone who made trouble!" he hissed. Alex was the sort who preferred to be a background person, knowing all things and all people without having to get himself into trouble. I ripped my arm out of his grip.

"I'm not making trouble. I'm just getting a closer look," I shot back. Then, I turned back and shoved my way past the other men standing around. Some of the men mildly protested my shoving, but most just ignored my presence. I glanced over my shoulder once and noticed that Alex had decided to follow.

"Typical," I muttered. Alex and I had been friends for about two years, and I usually took the lead while

Alex followed. It worked for me. The tyrrohn leader was leaving, observing the work of his men along the way. Deciding to follow him, but not be seen, I quickly ran behind the first burning house. The fire sprayed sparks at me. I ran past it and stayed behind the row of houses and reasonably sized yards. The tyrrohn leader took his time as he walked past all the property. I stopped at the edge of the last house on the row to watch him. It seemed apparent that he aimed to go into the woods. Alex caught up behind me; I could tell by his hard breathing. At that same moment, the tyrrohns joined their leader.

"They're going out of town. Come on," I told Alex.

"Adrian, if they see us, we get caught!" Alex warned. I glanced over my shoulder to see his face.

"Where's your sense of adventure?" I took off after them, dashing into the woods.

Tales of past tyrrohns in Chahcan were highlighted in history. Perhaps because they were interesting. Or, more probably, because the tyrrohns in Tolo, the capital, had become our leaders. Usually, these groups made a very noticeable entrance into the town, but made their way stealthily out of town to avoid being caught by current Chahcan rulers. These men weren't taking any precautions on their way out of town. The houses they had set on fire were like a massive, fiery line to the woods where they were heading. The way our men had just stood around watching them gave me the impression that the tyrrohns didn't need to hide.

They were well into the woods now, and I was just reaching the edge of it. Thankfully, the summer leaves and twigs were all mostly alive, and there were no forestry noises to give me away. The farther into Chahcan woods you go, the denser and darker it becomes. Light becomes scarce, except for where a few thin trees didn't have enough leaves to make a complete canopy. I continued to follow the tyrrohns into this thicker part of the forest until I could hear a river in the distance. They walked at ease, carrying their weapons in their hands, and glancing in all directions.

Suddenly, as I entered a lighter area of the woods, one of the tyrrohns whirled around to look in my direction. I was close enough to a tree to dive behind it and hope he hadn't seen me. I waited, hearing nothing for a while, and finally peered out around the tree.

"What?" I stepped fully into the clearing. I checked behind trees and did a 360. Nothing. The tyrrohns were gone. "They can't have disappeared that quickly. They weren't even running."

"You lost them?" Alex asked, abruptly appearing behind me. I jumped and spun around to face him.

"No," I retorted. Seeing Alex's incredulous look, I continued, "they disappeared. I'm telling you they were just right here a moment ago."

"Yeah, I'm not seeing an entire group of black-clad tyrrohns disappearing into the forest in the daylight," Alex pointed out.

"Well, what's your explanation?" I growled, frowning at him. "Ghosts?"

"Maybe. You never know," Alex insisted. In the two years that I had known Alex Ziegler, he had always had this thing for ghosts. One didn't have to wonder where he got it, knowing that he had many deserted houses surrounding his own. I shook my head at his agreement. These tyrrohns surely weren't ghosts, but I wasn't sure what I had just witnessed.

+ + + + + + +

Known as the 'poverty town,' Copper Ridge was occupied by the 'lower class' people. Just outside of this town was White Field, a village occupied mostly by 'upper class.' Directly on the line between these two towns was the property and mansion of a single, upper class man. People knew him as Bridge. I always assumed it was his last name. Bridge was known as a 'man of intelligence' and, like others in the country of Chahcan, had a small establishment for teaching boys. I had attended since I was twelve, a decision my parents had made.

Bridge's Mansion felt like something akin to organized chaos when I stepped in on Monday morning. Twenty-nine students, other than myself, were scuttling throughout the entryway, two hallways, and four rooms, explicitly opened for our benefit. On either side of both halls were bookcases. Each boy got one shelf to store their books, slate, and chalk.

I pushed through the boys to get to my shelf and reached up for the books I would need for our first lecture. Suddenly, a hand reached in front of my face and grabbed my slate.

"I'm going to need that," an irritating voice said. I whirled around.

"Give me that," I demanded.

"Why should I?" The guy glanced at me without so much as a smile. "I broke mine, only seems right I should take yours. Oh, hey, Falkner, I heard you were playing spy now and following tyrrohns." I wasn't surprised that Alex had spilled in the hearing range of Blake Rileder. Blake was a well-known bully. He and I had an unspoken misunderstanding: he got in my way, I pummeled him.

"Don't worry, Falkner. No one will miss you when you're gone. Can I get dibs on your skeleton?" Blake laughed. Clenching my fists, I leapt onto Blake, putting my knee on his chest. The slate went flying, as did both of our books. He grabbed my arms, attempting to hold me back. I wrenched my hands from him and punched his face. With his arms free, he returned the sting. I held down Blake's arms, but now neither of us could hit like we wished to.

Blake shouted one gruff word. Two of his 'friends', boys who hung around Blake because they thought they were in the same 'league' with him, came and pulled me up off him. A good group had now gathered to cheer on the fight, and they screamed at the help

Blake's 'friends' were giving him. Before Blake could get up, I slammed my knee into the back of the leg of the guy on the right, then I rolled over his back, dragging the second guy with me and slamming his body onto the ground.

Blake jumped on me, slamming his knee into my chest this time. I pushed with my arms and legs, slipped out, and kicked him in the face. He grabbed my leg and pulled me closer. I kicked with the other leg. Blake dropped my leg, and I stood back up. Blake and I charged at each other. Two other boys whom I didn't know came and tackled Blake's two helpers.

The next minute was a series of missed punches and kicks by Blake and me. Each missed swing made me want to feel my fist hit him and hurt him all the more. Blake got me first, and I quickly changed tactics. I grabbed Blake and picked him off the ground. I pinned him against a bookcase, making more books fall to the ground, and gained little satisfaction from the wince he gave. Before either of us could move, a loud shout broke into the fight. Cheers stopped as someone grabbed me and pulled Blake and me away. Our eyes were still locked.

*Hurt, I want to see Blake really hurt! That would feel like a victory!* I thought.

"That's enough! Get to the lecture." Bridge was by no means a small person. He usually had complete control of every situation with his commanding voice alone. Blake and I were his rare exceptions.

"I'll get revenge, Falkner," Blake said, darkly. He scooped up his books, and my slate, and walked away. I silently acknowledged his challenge from a distance. Revenge. It was something Blake had been looking to get for the last two years, ever since he had joined Bridge's lectures. I couldn't remember the last time I had lost a fight against Blake. For that reason alone, I had some existence inside of Bridge's Mansion, even though outside the walls, I was nonexistent.

+ + + + + + +

After lecture hours ended, Alex caught me while I was on my way out of Bridge's Mansion. He had attended for the same number of years I had; only I had never figured out why.

"Hey, Adrian!" he called. "Got time to spare tonight?" He sounded excited, which probably didn't mean anything good.

"What for?" I asked him.

"I've got some guys you should meet. And there's this girl..." Alex began. I didn't want to know.

"You know, you've got great commitment," I cut in sarcastically. Alex frowned. It was practically an insult. Alex had been seen with different girls every few months. The fact wasn't missed and even discussed in the Mansion despite Bridge's rules against rumors.

"You coming or not?" Alex asked, his tone harsher. I shook my head.

"Not. Athletics practice tonight, and I've got a ton of study for tomorrow," I said, glad to excuse myself from meeting Alex's group of guys and girl.

"You're always busy when I want you to meet a group of guys," Alex commented. "What's wrong? Afraid of crowds?" He grinned at the thought.

"No. Athletics could be a longstanding occupation, meeting your friends would last two minutes."

"You? Athletics? You'd sooner be involved in some war than athletics for life," Alex said. He was probably right, but I didn't let him get away with it.

"Yeah, right. Now get going, I'm going to be late. I'm not coming."

"Fine, later." Then, he ran from Bridge's property as if it had just burst into flames.

I spent the next hour doing what I considered my favorite thing: practicing, sweating, running till my legs felt numb. Even my arms hurt after this practice. The game of Chahcan was one of the most brutal sports in all of the Fallen Lands. We called it Ledo. The object was almost entirely lost in all the hitting, running, and snatching that went on. Still, when one had time to think about it, the object of the entire game was to get your team's ball to the other side of the field. Amidst the other team's efforts to keep you from your goal, one lost the ball more often than not. An excellent way to keep the ball moving down the field was to throw the ball to another player. I did this only when I knew I could get it into the hands of a teammate. I assumed a role of leadership when I got onto the field. I was the leader and was not led. I wasn't the only one vying for that position. There was another boy who thought he could do as well, but my determination always won over his. It's not that he didn't ever lead, just only sometimes.

One of the players, James, and I got along pretty well. He was my main target with his quick feet and great hands. He and I thought alike most of the time, which made our playmaking strong. The guys on my team weren't exactly my friends, but we respected each other enough to play together. That was all.

+ + + + + + +

Mom served supper late, as was very common in our family. She laid down plates with salad and a piece of chicken on each. I could see there was more chicken on her stove. Mom was just taking the usual precautions and not serving more than she must. That way, she could save anything that wasn't touched. The meal started in tranquility. All our meals had been this way, at least, for the last three years. I ate my chicken and stared at the salad; it wasn't a favorite of mine. I picked at it with my utensil for several minutes. Mom looked up and noticed me picking at the food.

"You can have another...uh, piece," Mom said quietly. I rose from the table. Mom had always been quiet, and she used to be very calm and easy-going. Even her hair was soft and a light blonde. Her blue eyes used to carry heartfelt compassion, but she wasn't that way anymore. She had changed her life schedule from staying home to working at some busy place in town. It had changed her outlook on life.

I grabbed another chicken piece and sat back down at the table, catching Dad's look on the way. He was staring at me with a disapproving scowl. I tried to ignore it and took a bite of my chicken. Dad had always been loud and busy. He hadn't changed at all; he still worked the same trade he did all those years ago. His black hair and green eyes were the same. I had inherited his black hair but gotten Mom's blue eyes. I finished the chicken piece and picked back up my utensil, wondering if the same trick would work, and I would get permission for another piece. Dad looked at me again and then sighed in frustration as he looked away. I dropped the utensil on the plate hard.

"What did I do this time?" I asked him. Dad sort of glanced at me.

"It has something to do with lectures today," he replied.

"What? I go to the lectures. I pay attention and know all the answers. Isn't that enough for anyone around here?" I fired at him.

"And in between lectures, you get caught fighting!" Dad shouted back at me.

"Yeah?" I stood up and threw the chair back. "You know where it comes from." Then, I fled the room. Behind me, I could hear Mom.

"Adrian," she called, then sighed. "You didn't let him finish his food."

"He started it!" Dad yelled. I paused just out of their sight, though I could still see them.

"You didn't have to speak. You only pick a fight!" Mom said, raising her voice. "You only make it worse."

"He doesn't respect us, anyway. We don't have any influence over him," Dad said.

"And whose fault is that? It's not his," Mom protested. "He's hurting just like us." Dad said something I couldn't make out. Then, Mom's voice called out again.

"No! John, come on..." Her voice faded as they walked away, leaving supper, yet again, on the table unfinished.

+++++++

Our family feuds always needed time to cool down and be 'forgotten.' By the time Ledo practice had ended the next day, it was only late afternoon. I slipped past our house quickly, hoping no one was watching. Sometimes neighbors were nosy. I decided to wander a bit. I would come back late and sneak up into my room without my parents knowing.

I had decided a long time ago that nothing was better than a long walk to nowhere—a long time to be alone and not focus on anything. I always came back home without knowing where I had gone, but it had always been the right place. I would hear but a few things, and the only thing that could draw me from my wandering was if another person joined me. Today, I walked through the woods, the thick, fading green forest surrounding me.

I could have been walking around for hours, or maybe it had not been that long. I didn't know, yet the sound of footsteps drew me from my wandering state. I instantly froze, listening to the noise of boots on the ground. The noise came closer, but I didn't move or dare to breathe. As suddenly as it had started, the crunching stopped, yet I remained unable to pry myself from the spot. I was alone and wanted to keep it that way. I had no idea where I was nor where I should walk to backtrack my progress. I looked overhead beyond the canopy of leaves and saw the faint trances left of the setting sun. Leaves shuffled from in front of me, and the soft sound of someone talking came from behind the brush. I turned around to leave.

*Thump.* I stumbled back in surprise. I had run headfirst into a tree that I hadn't seen.

"Ouch," came a voice now behind me, chuckling with amusement. "Are you okay?" I turned, embarrassed and angry, to see the intruder. It was a girl I didn't recognize. She was slender with wet hair hanging over her left shoulder.

"Fine," I said, my tone hinting sarcasm.

"Oh, good," she replied, smiling. Her smile was teasing, and her brown eyes sparkled. With her hair wet, I couldn't tell if it was brown or black.

"Adrian Falkner, right?" she asked in a cheery voice.

"Yeah, and who are you?" I wondered angrily.

"Helyn Thicket," the girl said, seeming to have ignored my tone. I'm sure the name should have meant something to me, but it didn't. Helyn continued, "Have you heard the news?"

"About what?"

"The fires caused by the tyrrohns," Helyn clarified. Not only was her voice cheerful, but it was soft, and each word seemed to flow perfectly together.

"Oh, sure. I was there when it happened." Helyn was immediately interested and asked what had happened. As cautiously as possible, I told what I saw and heard. After all, it was just Copper Ridge news. I reached the part where the tyrrohn leader was walking away and stopped.

"That's it?" Helyn inquired.

"What do you mean? It's not like I followed them to figure out where they were going," I objected. Helyn's big brown eyes stared at me, still sparkling with their teasing nature. I sighed. "Okay, so I followed them to figure out where they were going." Then, I launched into the last part of the story.

"Strange," she said, with a thoughtful look on her face, once I had finished.

"Everything in Copper Ridge is strange," I mentioned. "Compared to the rest of the world."

"Well, it's not just Copper Ridge. White Field is weird, too. Every landowner down there is full of tall tales and gossip. Have you ever been to White Field?" Helyn asked. I shook my head.

"I live down there, but my father doesn't raise crops or cattle for his living. The tales you'll hear down there though are just...absurd!" Helyn shook her head in disapproval. I realized that I had just slipped into a casual conversation with a girl who Alex would have loved to get to know.

"My father's into the trading business. What does your father do?" Helyn questioned brightly. I paused and frowned slightly, trying to answer this question.

"He owns a trading establishment, between Copper Ridge and the other towns as well as other countries overseas," I slowly replied. "He's gone a lot. He co-owns select parts of a ship company. He made a deal with the owner."

"Wow. Is your father rich?" Helyn inquired. My frown deepened. I had never been asked if Dad was rich. Of course, if we were, then he kept a pretty good secret.

"No," I told her. Then, muttered to myself, "not in the slightest."

"Neither is my father, really," she put in. I looked up at her.

"But, you live in White Field," I said, without thinking. Helyn smiled.

"It was my grandfather's place. Our house came as an inheritance. As well as all of our money," she explained.

"Oh."

"You know, White Field isn't that much different than Copper Ridge," Helyn said engagingly.

"How do you figure?"

"Well, they're both nobody towns. I mean, we don't have any influential people dropping by or passing through," Helyn pointed out.

"True. The Ruling Heads would do anything to skirt Copper Ridge and White Field," I agreed. Helyn laughed, a gentle, merry laugh. I now became aware that she had not used the term, but knew what it meant. We called any rich, influential person in Chahcan a 'Ruling Head.' It was like a combined title and insult.

"We aren't allowed to call them 'Ruling Heads' in White Field, or anywhere else for that matter," Helyn noted.

"Have you been to any of the other towns?" I asked. She nodded.

"My family has traveled a lot in the past. We lived in Tolo, Kriff, and Vainus before settling in White Field," Helyn replied.

I could practically see a map in my head of Chahcan. Copper Ridge and White Field were the south-east towns. Iron Cap and Kriff were in the north-west, sitting in the mountain range. The capital, Tolo, consumed the entire west coast. Chahcan's twin towns were port cities lying directly opposite of each other; Veaus in the north-east and Vainus in the south-west.

Helyn went on, "We continue to travel a little each year. Of course, in Tolo, you see Ruling Heads passing by all the time." I smiled at her use of the term. "They act like they were kings of old, with servants, horses, and carriages all making a big procession down busy cobblestone streets."

"As good as the tyrrohns," I snapped. Helyn shrugged. She threw her head back to look at the sky. The sun was gone now, and with it, the light. I figured it was about seven, which wasn't late enough for me to go home yet.

"I guess I'd better start the trek back to White Field," Helyn said, in that cheery voice that had started the conversation.

"Okay," I said as she turned to go. She gave me a wave. I turned to leave. Thump. I had run headfirst into that same tree again.

"Ouch," Helyn exclaimed, chuckling again. "I'm not sure if I should say the tree likes you or you like it."

"Well, it's nothing on my part," I groused.

# CHAPTER TWO

# The Unforgotten Things

I had a love-hate relationship with our neighbor's pet rooster. Although that obnoxious bird did wake me up on time for weekdays, the thing didn't understand weekends. Saturday morning, I woke to the annoying sound.

*Er, er, er, er, er-rck, rck, rck, rck.*

In truth, the rooster didn't know how to crow, even after all these years, and so it turned out more like a short crow, a sputter, and then a cough. I pulled a pillow over my head and groaned. The rooster repeated his 'crow' twice more and then finally choked off.

I lay back in bed and stared at the ceiling. I could hear my parents' footsteps on the second floor. I assumed they were getting ready to leave. They both worked seven to ten hours, seven days a week. I had no idea what they did in all that time they spent away from the house, but I didn't care. Somehow in between working, Mom found enough time to cook meals and leave them for me to eat when I needed them. The footsteps faded as they walked down the stairs, and I heard the door open and close behind them. I was alone. I knew that I would need to show up at the field for the Ledo game today, but that wasn't until the afternoon. So, I had plenty of time to lie in bed.

*Er, er, er, er, er-rck, rck, rck, rck.*

I groaned once again and got up from the bed. Crossing the room, I slammed my window fully shut. I couldn't remember why I had opened it in the first place. Throwing on some casual clothes, I took off for the woods again. I started heading in the general direction of center-town, but soon forgot where I was. I was wandering, but for some reason, a thought interrupted me from my condition.

*I wonder if Helyn might happen along,* I thought. Then, I posed, *what made you think of that, Adrian?*

Subconsciously, I told myself that I had enjoyed her conversation. Soon enough, I slipped into my wandering state. When I decided to figure out where I was, I found myself on the top of the hill that led down to White Field and all the lavish homes and fields beyond.

It would have been a peaceful scene of everlasting green fields, large houses, and animals grazing peacefully. Except for the fires spread over the fields and the large gathering of people in the area below me. Never had I ever a want to enter White Field, but now I made my way to join the group. As soon as I got close, I could hear the voices. I pushed my way through the crowd so I could see the men in black, their leader, and the men who challenged him.

"I believe I've made my intentions quite clear by now." The loud voice came from the one who had been leading the men in black, the tyrrohn leader.

"We can't give you what you want! But let it be known, if we could, we would still refuse to give up information," one bold man from the crowd said. He stood at a face-off with the leader. The enraged leader grabbed the unarmed man and forced him to his knees, holding his arms behind his back. The leader pressed a sword to the man's neck. The move was so fluent the tyrrohn seemed but a black mass.

"Even at the cost of your life? Is it that important to you?" the leader asked.

"If these fighters are everything you say they are and have stopped you from both finding them and halting them from helping the people, then they are worth protecting for the good of the people." The man bent as the tyrrohn pushed the blade more firmly against his neck.

"You're sure?" came the challenge.

"No," the man answered boldly, "because cause all I have is your word to go on, and I cannot help but wonder if what you say is true or false. You aren't the most reliable source."

"And what gives you that idea?"

"Let me put it this way: should we believe you, who has burned our houses and fields? Or maybe, believe the words of One much greater, whose words and actions have never been anything but love?"

The man's words confused me, but the leader gave a satisfied nod. He hit the man with the hilt of his sword, and the man fell to the ground in pain, but not unconscious.

"You should have been more careful, fighter," the leader spat. "Take him with us. Our master will deal with him accordingly." Someone in the crowd screamed. With one motion, several of the men in black came and picked up the man, holding him hostage with weapons. I glared at the leader as he turned to address the rest of us.

"The wrong of this man is doubting that I mean serious business is carrying out the orders given to me. I will find every one of his kind and deal with them. You who are associated with them will suffer at the hands of my master." The leader then walked as if he was going to leave.

Anger flooding through me, I acted before I could think. I ran at the leader and grabbed his black clothes that flew in the hot wind. Wrapping them quickly around my hands, I pulled on them and tripped the unsuspecting leader. He dropped his sword as he went down and turned to glare at me. Grabbing his sword once again, he made to swing at me, but I jumped to the side and easily avoided the swing. The tyrrohn leader stood.

"You dare defy me?" he mocked. "You against my army of men and my skill so superior to yours."

"Skill in making fire, no one can doubt, but what skill is required to fall?" I retorted. His men rushed up behind me, like a dark cloud surging across the sky.

"Never mind, men, ignore this one." The leader walked closer to me. With one quick motion, he struck me down, and then he stood over me. "Pathetic." With that word, he led the way out of White Field. I glared after him. A cold, aching feeling drew my attention to my hands. I turned my hands over, wondering at the strange rushing feeling that pulsed through my fingers and up my arms. Again, I looked up to stare after the tyrrohns, but they were gone.

"What's going on here?" I murmured to myself.

+++++++

I walked down the cobblestone street, heading for Alex's place. The Ledo game was over, and I had agreed to spend some time at his home. My hands and arms felt normal now, including a few new bruises from Ledo. I turned off the main street and onto a small unnamed road that had a good number of houses built right along the road. Halfway down the road, the cobblestone pattern stopped, and it was all dirt and small rocks.

I was walking in the space that served as the pathway to Alex's home, in between two of the larger houses on the street, when something dropped behind me. I quickly turned to see what it was.

A rough hand covered my mouth, and then I was pulled against the side of one of the houses.

"About time you showed up," the person said behind me in a hushed tone, as he removed his vise-like grip. The voice definitely belonged to a young male. I took a step away from him. "Here, take this." He held out a small, thick book. I reached to take it as instructed, though very confused. Suddenly, he pulled it back.

"On one condition: don't tell anyone the location," he spoke with urgency. I stepped farther away from the wall and the person. I looked him over carefully, but couldn't see much of his figure or his facial features, a dark cloak covered that. He was tall and maybe older than me. His voice, though it had a sense of secrecy and urgency, still hinted at playful and boyish. My first thought had been he was part of the tyrrohns, but something told me that this boy couldn't possibly be one of them. He once again held out the book. Though somewhat reluctantly, I accepted it, afraid of what he might do if I denied the book. I looked at the cover.

*Fighters from Ancient Days*, it read.

*A history book?* I looked back up at the person who still stood in front of me.

"Just don't tell anyone the location," he repeated.

"Why? What location? Why are you handing me a history book?" I asked. I must have spoken too loud for the mysterious boy because he took two steps toward me and covered my mouth again with one of his hands.

"You'd do best to read the book," he said. He turned to leave. Glancing back over his shoulder, the boy added, "and, Adrian Falkner, you mean more to the fighters than you'll ever know." Then, the mysterious boy disappeared in the fading light.

*The fighters? This boy is a part of the fighters that the tyrrohns want to draw out? And why does he know my name?*

I hid the history book on Alex's porch before going in. I didn't want to give him the idea that I had brought studies to his place. We never did studies together because it didn't matter whether the kid did well in them or not. His parents thought he was perfect either way. Taking a deep breath to calm rising anger, I knocked on the door and stepped into his house.

+ + + + + + +

I came back from Alex's place late, and the streets were already dark. With the promise that I would return it, Alex had let me use one of his parents' lanterns. I was in no hurry to be home, hoping that my parents would be in their room by the time I got back. So, my steps were slow, and the light shone only on the cobblestone street directly in front of me. I had been at Alex's place for hours, but I couldn't remember what we had done. As I thought about it, I couldn't place why Alex and I were friends. We were total opposites. I shook the thought, not going any further. A sudden motion caused me to look left and then regret that I had. Standing beside a building was the shadow of a man. Other than his face, he was completely black, and his body had no specific form.

I would have looked away except the eyes, which glowed with an unusual light, held me in place. After a long minute, I shook away from the stare and took a cautious step toward the figure. It stood as still as a statue. Raising my lantern, I walked toward the figure. As soon as the beam came to the spot where the figure stood, it disappeared. With curiosity, I pulled the lantern away from the place. To my amazement, the figure was still standing there. Disturbed by the appearance, I hurried to get off the streets.

+++++++

The neighbor's rooster forgot to crow and choke on Monday morning. I woke up late and ended up at Bridge's Mansion without breakfast. One of those 'hate' days. I avoided contact with any people in between lectures. I didn't look for Blake, and I didn't pay much attention to Alex. Finally, the lectures ended, and I made a quick dash to get off of Bridge's property. Ledo practice restored some of my good humor. What made getting hit and bruised, losing a ball, and fighting every last inch to get to the other side of the field good? I couldn't explain it. At any rate, I turned to leave the grounds in a slightly better mood.

"Adrian Falkner!" The voice stopped me. I didn't have a hard time knowing who spoke. I turned and saw Helyn Thicket making her way toward me. I could now clearly see that her flowing, wavy hair matched her brown eyes.

"Is it true that you saw what the tyrrohns have done in White Field?" she asked, her voice low. I frowned.

"Who..." I began. She shook her head.

"No one you would know. They know of you, though," Helyn said.

"I believe that. It seems a lot of people know me, and I don't know them," I growled, exaggerating the statement because of my frustration. Helyn tilted her head in curiosity.

"What do you mean?" she asked.

"Never mind."

"What? Can't you tell me?" I shook my head.

"It's nothing."

"Yes, it is something. Who else knows you? Who don't you know?" Helyn pressed.

"I don't know a lot of people," I answered evasively.

"Oh, come on. Tell me."

"Won't you just leave it alone?"

"You brought it up," Helyn pointed out. I huffed.

"Fine!" I gave up.

Then, I told her about the mysterious messenger who had given me the history book.

Helyn tried to hide a smile with her hand. "Well, Adrian, I think you need to read that book," she said mysteriously.

+ + + + + + +

I slipped into the house, closing the door softly. I made a dash for my room, hearing someone in the kitchen.

"Adrian?" Mom called. I was two steps from the door, and Mom couldn't see me yet. Before I could decide to race into my bedroom and lock the door before Mom could see me, she rounded the corner.

"You are home," she stated. I turned slowly to face her. "I expected you for dinner." Once again, I had lingered in town and the woods before coming home. It was becoming a habit.

"I wasn't hungry," I muttered. Mom dropped her head.

"Yes, well, your father won't be around for a while," Mom said. "He's on a business trip."

"Big surprise," I said, under my breath. Mom's head shot back up.

"What did you say?" She didn't wait for an answer. "Look, Adrian, I know you and he are not on great terms, but he cares for you."

"Does he really? He has a great way of showing it," I retorted sarcastically.

"It's not like that…" Mom tried.

"He's always gone. And when he is here, he's always angry at me."

"It…he's always tried hard to be the father you need. It's just been harder for the last several years," Mom said, struggling with words.

"Everything's been harder for the last several years," I corrected. Mom nodded, her eyes filled with tears.

"I know, and I'm sorry things happened the way they did, but…I couldn't stop them from happening," Mom apologized.

"But you had a choice…" I pressed. Mom shook her head, and the tears spilled down her cheeks.

"Not really," she said.

"You haven't even tried since then!" I accused. I wanted Mom to deny it, but she only kept crying and nodded in agreement. I grew instantly enraged beyond anything before.

"I can't believe you!" I screamed at her. Then, I stormed into my room and locked the door. I exhaled forcefully and plopped on my bed. The room was dark because I had forgotten to light a kerosene lamp. The moon gave off very little light through the curtains that covered my window.

Thoughts churned through my mind like a tornado. *What do I care about his stupid business trip? He's always on one of those. What difference does it make? Our house isn't peaceful, whether he's here or not! Can't Mom just see that it doesn't matter and leave me alone? Why does she have to try to inform me about what they do? Mom knows it makes me angry. Yet, she does it all the time. Why?*

I laid back on the bed and clenched my fists. My own words hit me in the face: everything's been harder for the last several years. I clenched my jaw. The only one to blame for that, besides my parents, was my former older brother, Morro. He wasn't dead; I had mentally disowned him. My mind formed a picture of him, and, when I closed my eyes, I found myself practically staring at his features; black hair, which spilled into his dark eyes, in complete contrast to his pale face. He was six years my elder and, when I was little, he had been my role model.

As an easily influenced ten-year-old kid, Morro had gotten me to do his dirty work: stealing weapons and illegal liquor from the homes in White Field. I later found out that he took it to a group of tyrrohns. Over and over again, I stole, passed the items on to Morro, and he took them to the tyrrohns. Then, one night, everything changed.

I had snuck inside a White Field home, grabbed the weapons, and slipped back out the window. With this accomplished, I had run straight into an old alley between two abandoned buildings and met Morro there. That night, the sight of Morro in his dark, hooded cloak in that alley was frightening to me. Morro took the items, but I glanced wildly around.

"You betraying me?" Morro had hissed in my ear. Before I had a chance to answer, men leapt into the alley, calling to us. Morro had forced me to run. I had no intention of getting caught, and wound my way toward home, down a particular alley which I knew led directly back. After a long minute, though, I glanced back and noticed that Morro wasn't following. He was running in the opposite direction. I had stopped running, standing dumbfounded as the militia caught up to me and left Morro to escape town.

I groaned and rose from my bed. Pain coursed through my body like an internal wound. Why had Morro left me? Me, just a ten-year-old boy who had done all he ever asked? Why leave me with the record of a thief and tyrrohn ally? These were questions which, I assumed, would never get answered. That had all happened six years ago and was only the beginning of my family's problems.

I sighed. I needed something to get my mind off family problems. I knew I wasn't going to sleep with my mind a storm of questions and irate thoughts. I needed something to do. I looked over at my desk and saw the history book that the mysterious fighter had given me. It was sitting there, covered in other papers, as it had been since I had brought it home a day ago. I jumped off the bed with a sudden vigor and sat down at my desk. I pushed the papers off the book and opened it.

The first page had words so tiny I didn't even try to read it. The next few pages were just a bunch of randomly scribbled lines, dedicating the book to unknown persons. I finally found the first page I could read. I read quickly, my eyes scanning the words faster than I could comprehend them. It didn't take long to note that this wasn't a history book; it was full of strange poems and proverbs. I only read as far as the first two stanzas. Their words caught me off guard. I stared at them until they blurred.

+ + + + + + +

I raced off the main road and down the unnamed street that led to Alex's place. Still running, I rang the doorbell and then launched myself into the house, slamming the door shut behind me. Quickly locating the stairs, I went up two at a time, making it to Alex's room in record time. I didn't knock, but rather the door slammed shut, announcing me. Alex sat at his desk, looking at some indistinct object.

"Did you bring back the lantern?" he asked in a distant tone. I threw the lantern on his bed.

"Yeah, saw something weird on the streets the other night, too."

"Oh?" Alex sounded only half interested. Whatever he was doing at his desk seemed to be taking up much of his attention. I told him about the dark figure anyway. About halfway through my description, I caught his full attention.

"Adrian, are you trying to tell me you saw a ghost?" Alex asked, with some enthusiasm. I sighed.

"I don't believe in ghosts," I told him.

"Whatever." Alex turned his attention back to his desk and the object on it.

"Wait, I have something else to show you." I took the book and slammed it down on his desk. Alex looked up.

"Why did you bring a history book to my house?" he asked. I shook my head and opened it.

"Read the first page," I told him.

"Are you serious? I'm not reading that history book!" Alex protested.

"It's not a history book. Overlook the title and read the page," I insisted. Alex was far from belief. "Read it," I urged. He gave me an unimpressed look and read it.

"'What will begin as a flame, will ultimately consume

what began with a few, will conquer you;

Your past is not the future; it is your end

because they will overtake you with fear.'"

Alex looked up at me with confusion. "What about it?" he asked.

"The tyrrohns," I answered. Alex reread the passage, and it suddenly dawned on him.

"You mean, this book's predicting the future?" Alex was instantly impressed. It had taken me a long time, but I had finally understood most of the riddle. The first flames had been only a house, but then they had consumed fields. The tyrrohns had grown in number as well and had overtaken the people with fear.

"Cool," Alex said, then he read the next one. I had a feeling his 'cool' was about to change.

"'Stuck in your fear, the power will take you;
Your soul will be taken, your life diminished,
and your ignorance will open the Gates of Suffering.'"

Alex's face suddenly turned sour. "Well, that's encouraging," he said, almost sarcastically. I had to agree it wasn't exactly what you would want to be told your future is. "Is the whole book this depressing? I mean, if we die on the first page, what happens for the rest of the future?" Alex flipped through the book, trying to read the other lines.

"That's just it," I explained. "None of the others make sense."

"But we can't just die with this much of the book left," Alex exclaimed, astonished. "No way am I going to die! I still have the best years of my life to live." It was my turn to give him an unimpressed look. What were 'the best years of your life' when you were sixteen years old? He didn't see my look; he was too busy reading the other sentences that seemed a bunch of random words that didn't go together.

"There's some way to prevent it from happening, right? We can't be dead. Maybe, we aren't dead, but only sort of dead. You know, like in those old stories,"

Alex said, looking to me for back up. I had none for him.

"Alex," I objected, "that's not even possible. You've been listening to way too many ghost stories." Alex shrugged and looked at the book. He slammed it shut and shoved it back at me.

"Why did you bother to show me that? Now I have to walk around with the weight of knowing I'm going to die hanging over me. Oh, come on. There's gotta be a way to prevent that from happening, right?" Alex asked. I shrugged.

"I don't have the answers," I replied aloud. Then, added mentally, *although, I know someone who might.*

# CHAPTER THREE

## The Ache Inside

*Er, er, er, er, er-rck, rck, rck, rck.*

I rolled over in the bed without opening my eyes.

"One of these days," I moaned to myself, "that bird will end up as meat on my plate."

I tried to convince myself that I could stay in bed, but the rooster insisted. I groaned and got up from my bed. I had slept in my clothes, but I figured they were clean enough. So, I grabbed my stuff and the book and raced out the door. It wasn't the first time I had decided to skip Bridge's lectures and take off for the woods.

This time, though, I was walking for White Field. I traversed the terrain quickly, knowing the way like the back of my hand. I was nearly halfway there when I heard a shout. I froze, looking around for the person. For a minute, nothing presented itself.

Then, a person ran into view, shouting: "there's another one! Grab him, men!" Four other men came into view and ran toward me. I sprinted in the opposite direction. By their black clothing and weapons, I could tell they were part of the tyrrohns. I ducked and jumped through the forestry, but no smart trick I tried threw them off my trail.

All of a sudden, another person jumped out of the woods and was running beside me.

"This way!" a feminine voice yelled, grabbing my arm and pulling me faster. Since she obviously wasn't a tyrrohn, I figured it was a good idea to let her lead. Somehow, I managed to keep up and running. The person pulled me into dense forestry. Moving quickly, she stopped and pulled up a door hidden on the ground.

"Get in!" My rescuer shoved me in and quickly jumped down, pulling the door over us. We heard shouts from the men above us. For a moment, I thought they might find us, but they ran on till we couldn't hear them anymore. Suddenly, I recognized the person who was beside me in the small space.

"Helyn?" She flashed me a smile and shook her wavy brown hair out of her face.

"And we run into each other again, Adrian Falkner," she teased.

"Good to see you, too," I said, smiling back at her. "And your timing couldn't have been any better." She shrugged it off.

"What I want to know is why the tyrrohns were following you in the first place," Helyn stated.

"You're asking me?" I queried, looking around us. "What are we in, and how did you know it was here?"

"It's an old cellar, used to hide people and, more commonly, canned food," Helyn explained, ignoring my second question.

She looked out of the cellar, surveying the surrounding forest.

"I think we're safe now," she said. We climbed out of the cellar. "Did you read the book?" Helyn asked.

"Yeah, I did." I explained what I had read, and the conclusions Alex and I had made. Helyn laughed.

"You almost have it, just not quite," she clarified. "The book isn't about the future. It's about the past."

"The past?" I asked, confused. "Then how..." I wasn't quite sure what I wanted to ask.

"How come it matches with now and seems to predict that we're going to die?" she finished for me.

"Yeah, that," I agreed.

"Well, the truth is you've already died," Helyn said. She tried to smother a laugh at my shocked expression. "Not literally, Adrian, figuratively."

"Figuratively, how?" I posed.

"You're living now, so what happens when you die?" she asked. I wasn't getting it.

"You either go to Heaven or Hell," she answered her question.

"And what determines where we go?"

"It's your choice." This response caught me off guard.

"I get to choose?" I clarified.

"Yes, we get to choose to believe in Jesus Christ, God's Son, as our only door to heaven...or reject His righteousness and hope that our actions are good enough to get us to heaven," Helyn explained. "God has given each man free will to choose his path, even though He already knows what you will choose."

"Okay, but I don't understand. How is it that I've already died?" I asked, then added, "uh, figuratively speaking."

"Since the fall of man, we've all been born with a sinful nature, and therefore we have no way to get to Heaven. Because," she said quickly, "our sin has separated us from God. So, we were all condemned to die and perish in Hell."

"Wait, hold on. The fall of man?" I asked. Bridge's lectures had covered 'superstitious religions' before, but Helyn's words were going over my head. Helyn smiled knowingly.

"Stick with the conversation at hand. That's another whole day's worth of material." Helyn said. Then, she prodded, "so, you are figuratively dead because…?" I thought another moment, trying to bring to my mind of all her words for the idea.

"Um, so it's not that we've really died, but we were already dead because we couldn't make things right?" I puzzled.

"You got it!" Helyn encouraged.

"I guess. So, what changes that fact? How do we, you know, stop ourselves from dying?" I asked. Helyn seemed to consider her answer.

"That's a long answer," she finally said. I gave her a look of expectation. She shook her head. "Not here. We need to get to somewhere safe, someplace where the tyrrohns won't find us." Then, she walked away. I followed right behind her.

We walked through a seemingly endless forest. Occasionally, the sound of running water came, but it faded just as quickly. Helyn appeared to be following an almost undefined path, marked by small cuts in a tree here and there or a specific log over which she had to jump. I could tell only by the way she studied marks on the trees or counted the fallen logs in certain places.

Helyn didn't take any of that time to talk; instead, she seemed to enjoy the silence. We walked for close to an hour. The forest became less dense and thinned out into many clearings. Finally, a strange noise interrupted the silence; a humming. The longer we walk, the more pronounced the sound became, until it reminded me of human voices. Just as I opened my mouth to say something, Helyn really broke the silence.

"Here we are," Helyn said with a satisfied tone. I rounded the group of trees that blocked me from seeing what she did and gaped at the sight.

Now, as far as I could see, there were tents of every shape and size erected in uneven rows. Like a small village, the place had an orderliness to it and was swarming with thousands of people. Men and women walked from one place to another and stood in groups to talk. Children scurried in and around the tents, laughing and playing with sticks and balls.

This explained the humming sound. I quickly noticed that all the men near us were armed.

"Welcome to the home of the fighters known as the Defencio Veritas," Helyn smiled, gesturing to the place before us.

"The what?" I asked.

"Defencio Veritas. It means the Defense of Truth."

"These are the secret fighters the tyrrohns are looking for? And this is their home?" I asked.

"Yup," Helyn cheerily answered. She started forward, walking between two rows of tents, and I followed.

"Well, how come the tyrrohns haven't found them?" I asked.

"The Enclave is an itinerant home for the Defencio Veritas. They move about the woods of Chahcan frequently, and sometimes they have two or three locations. After all, with eighty percent of Chahcan being forests, they've got a lot of space to work with."

"How is moving even possible?" I queried.

"Well, one family can collapse their tent in eight minutes. It's like building the walls in Nehemiah," Helyn explained. "With each family responsible for their tent, we can get it done in record time. If need be, we can be packed up and moving out in half an hour."

"Seriously?" I gasped.

"I wouldn't say it if it wasn't true," Helyn laughed at my incredulity. She went on, "When the Defense moves, they leave small signs that mark the path for us to follow." Suddenly, my eyes were taken off the place around me and fastened on her face.

"You're one of the secret fighters?" I exclaimed. Helyn gave me her teasing smile.

"You're just now figuring that out?" she shot back. I nodded slowly. The thought of the tyrrohns wanting to harm Helyn or anyone like her was almost inconceivable. What could she have done that was worse than the tyrrohns themselves? I turned my gaze back to the rows of tents, campfires, and people we were passing.

"So, you all live out here permanently?" I asked.

"Most of the Defenders do. Some, like me, have homes in which they are safe at Copper Ridge and White Field. Now, pick up your pace. There are some people here who want to meet you," Helyn playfully commanded.

"Me?"

"I might have mentioned you once or twice," Helyn said mischievously. I wondered if that answered the question of how the mysterious fighter had known my name.

We picked up our pace, weaving through the nigh endless rows of tents. The secret fighters gave us passing glances, but in general, they all seemed to be busy. They weren't in a hurry, nor were they idle; they just walked and worked with a purpose. At last, we reached the tent Helyn was looking for. It was enormous, towering over my head by several feet, and its topmost pole was stuck between two branches of the overhanging tree.

"Come in," Helyn motioned me eagerly into the place.

"But, I..." Helyn laughed at me as she grabbed my arm and pulled me in. Seven men sat inside on the ground, talking to each other in low tones. There was one man in the corner with a blank stare, leaning against a supporting beam. They were all dressed similarly; simple, drab colored, every day clothes of Chahcan design. Like me, each wore a plain, cotton shirt, and slightly baggy pants tucked into boots. However, each of them had a weapon at their side. One of the men seated on the ground turned from the conversation as we approached.

"Ah, Helyn, you never fail on a mission," the man said. Then, he turned to me. "Welcome, Adrian."

"Hi," I said, looking at Helyn for an introduction. She didn't disappoint.

"Adrian, the Seven Leaders of the Defencio Veritas." Now, all the men looked our way.

"Allow me to introduce you," the first leader began, standing to his feet, and strapping his sword to his side in one fluent motion. "Leaders, this is Adrian Falkner, as some of you might know. Adrian, these are the seven; Robert, Abel, Will, Titus, Howard, and Colin Burlance."

Each man stood as their name was called out, picking up their weapons also.

"And the one that he failed to mention was, naturally, himself," Colin Burlance said in a jovial voice. He was tall, broad-shouldered, with a big smile, blond hair, and bright blue eyes. "Adrian, meet Edmund Naric," Colin introduced, chuckling and waving a hand toward the one he was presenting. "Oh, forgive me, Commander Edmund Naric. I forget that he is the commander of our forces." The commander sighed and shook his head.

"You can address me as Naric," he said. I nodded. "Did you have a hard time getting him here?" Naric spoke to Helyn. Her eyes sparkled with fun.

"It wasn't too hard," she started. "I mean, he's pretty slow. It took him until two minutes ago to figure out my involvement with you all."

"Yeah. Are you going to keep insulting me? Or maybe, you can explain why you're showing me all this?" I fired back. Helyn gave me a playful look.

"We've been stalking you for a whole year, trying to find some way to get you involved. Just don't ask why," she challenged.

"Why?" I asked, then couldn't help but grin. Helyn laughed.

"Okay. Because you are important to the Defense's win against our enemy."

"Me?" I pointed at myself. Naric nodded. "Why me?" A dread crept into my being as I wondered if my past with Morro was about to be brought up.

"Well," Colin added in, "let's just say, Providence led us to know that our enemy is targeting you."

"Who is your enemy?" I asked.

"That's just it," Helyn mentioned. "We don't know who he is exactly. We know where he's been but beyond that...well, it's scattered. He's kept himself hidden...waiting for you." I wondered if their enemy came in the form of a rooster who couldn't crow.

"So, if he's targeting me...what does this have to do with you guys?" I inquired.

"He attacked us first, demanding we hand you over," Naric explained. "We had no clue at the time who you were. Then, the Lord spoke to us, telling us that He was going to use you to bring about the victory."

"I don't get it. Once he figured out you didn't know me, why didn't the enemy just leave you alone? Why are you still fighting him?"

"Because he knows you are meant to come here. It's your quest, Adrian," Helyn explained in a more serious tone. The atmosphere in the tent stilled. "You only have to be willing to take the quest," she added. Her tone surprised me.

"What do you mean?"

"It isn't going to be easy. You'll face things that will turn you from the goal. You have to train hard and know the Scriptures. You have to be willing to give up everything you knew. After the quest, well, life just isn't the same," Helyn said. She seemed to imply that she knew what one of these quests held.

"You have to be ready for your life to change completely."

*The last thing I want is for my life to change any more than it already has,* I thought.

As I processed what Helyn had said, the tent flap flew open, and another man burst in.

"Commander Naric, tyrrohns have been spotted four miles from our location. Should we pass the word to relocate?" the man reported. Helyn gasped.

"How could I forget? Commander Naric, they saw Adrian in the woods," she said in a hurry.

"Yeah, and it seems they're determined to get me," I added. Naric addressed the messenger.

"Yes, pass the word. Keep on high alert," he ordered. Naric turned to us. "Helyn, get him out of here. The tyrrohns can't find him here." Helyn nodded. She grabbed my arm again and pulled me out of the tent. We ran from the secret fighters' home.

"Are the tyrrohns allied with your enemy?" I called ahead. Helyn shrugged, palms up.

"Let's just say they're not good news," she answered.

"Where are we going?" I wondered.

"Back to Copper Ridge, where you'll be safe," Helyn replied. She turned her head back to look at me, signaling with one finger across her lips that we needed to be silent. We didn't talk the whole way back to Copper Ridge. Standing on an abandoned road, we caught our breath.

"Sorry if I've sprung everything on you too quickly," Helyn apologized quietly. "You know, The Enclave, the fighters, the quest. There's a sense of urgency with anything involving the Defense."

"Yeah, it was a little sudden," I admitted. "But if it answers everything about what has been going on recently, then I don't have too many objections. I'm just not sure I can get myself caught up in a war."

"I understand, but just remember that if our enemy gets his way, then he'll take over all of Copper Ridge and White Field," Helyn said. "Anyway, keep reading that book."

"I don't know," I said, giving her a skeptical look. "It's gotten me into some strange circumstances recently. I'm not sure how much more I can take."

"Probably more than you think," Helyn maintained. "I have to go, or I won't make it back to White Field in time. Consider the quest. The book might even hold some answers. And, please, don't tell anyone the location of The Enclave."

+ + + + + + +

I made it out of the house the next morning and to Bridge's Mansion just before Bridge called for the first lecture. My absence yesterday wasn't noted. The lectures dragged, and my mind wandered. Once they ended, I quickly made my way to the field. James met me the minute I was on the field.

"Hey, Adrian. What happened to you yesterday?" he called. I shrugged. Practice finished two hours later, and afterward, I decided to head home.

I slipped inside and to my room. Kicking my shoes across the floor, I sat at the desk and opened the mysterious book that had been given to me. I glanced over all the words until I came across one at the back of the book, which caught my intrigue.

*"'Called into battle by some great light;*
*Called into belief by your own past;*
*Called into victory by defeat.'"*

Looking closer at the words, I realized that they were of a different hand than the rest of the book. The ink was splattered more carelessly, and the words fell from their original line. It appeared that they were added more recently. The last words confused me the most.

"Victory gained through defeat? How does that make sense? Those are like, totally opposite." I had inherited the bad habit of talking to myself out loud, speaking my thoughts. It was one of the few things Dad and I shared in common. "Maybe…" I started to think.

"Adrian?" I slammed the book shut and turned to look at the door where Mom stood, her head poking into my room. "What are you doing?"

"Uh, just…just reading a history book," I answered, hoping she would let it go at that. Mom walked into the room.

"Can I see it?" she inquired. I shrugged and slid the book toward her, acting as if it didn't matter to me. Mom picked up the book and scanned a page or two. I hoped it made as little sense to her as it did to me. Mom set the book down on the desk again.

"O-kay. Are you coming down to eat?" The question was rhetorical.

"Oh, yeah, just give me a minute," I said. Mom consented and walked away. I grabbed the book, pulled it in front of me again, and opened it to the same spot with the additional note. For some reason, the words seemed to call me.

"Called into battle," I mused. My mind instantly conjured an image of the tyrrohn leader standing over me, shaking his head and calling me 'pathetic.' Then, it went back further, to the time when I had been called a 'tyrrohn ally.' That title should have belonged to Morro instead of me. My breathing deepened, and I clenched my fists. The quest offered by the Defense involved defeating these tyrrohns and the man behind them.

"I'll do it," I muttered, rising to my feet. "I'll take the quest and show that tyrrohn a thing or two. I am not an ally!"

"Adrian!" Mom called. I closed the book once again with my mind made up and ran down the stairs. I joined Mom at the table, devouring the chicken, beans, and corn on the plate. Mom and I ate in silence. I think we were both happy to have a quiet meal.

Once the meal was finished, Mom rose and cleared our plates, putting them in the sink. She would wash them later, or tell me to. I excused myself from the table and went to the door.

"Where are you going?" Mom asked, looking up from the sink.

"Uh, Alex's house," I said hesitantly. I hoped she wasn't about to give me the dish chore. Mom simply nodded and began the dishwashing herself. I bolted out the door before Mom had a chance for second thoughts. I reached Alex's house an hour later, just as the last rays of the setting sun sank below the horizon. I knocked on the door, walked in, and made my way to Alex's room. Alex's parents were very nonchalant about me coming and going without notice. I wasn't even sure they knew I ever came over. I found Alex lying on his bed, reading a book, which he dropped as I came in.

"If you brought that book again..." Alex began to threaten. I shook my head.

"No, I brought the answer to the book," I said, jumping on his bed. He sat up and waited. "It's not a book about the future. It's about the past."

"Wow, that all? So, we aren't going to die, we're already dead," Alex said, picking up on some sarcasm.

"Yeah," I agreed. Alex's astonished expression told me that he hadn't expected that answer. "Figuratively speaking, anyway." Now he gave me a confused look.

"I am so unimpressed with your translation of that book," Alex said. I rapidly explained what Helyn had told me, only in my own words, and leaving out who had told me. "This is a religious book?" Alex frowned.

"Maybe," I shrugged.

"Okay, let me get this straight: we're dead and have no hope of becoming alive," Alex summed up. I nodded.

"Pretty much."

"You're finding this amusing, Adrian. This isn't funny. First, we're going to die. Now we are dead." Alex moved his hands in a series of animated motions, which showed his exasperation more than his words. I decided not to answer him. A long silence fell over us. Alex picked back up his book and appeared to be reading. Finally, he dropped it back in his lap.

"So, if we're already dead, wouldn't that make us ghosts?" he asked.

"You would say that," I groaned, rising to leave.

"Come on, you're the one that saw a ghost figure on the streets," Alex argued.

"Alex, that figure wasn't a ghost!"

"Whatever!" Alex flopped back on his bed. I shook my head and left the house. Without the intrigue of a quest, the book's concepts were lost on Alex.

*I guess I'll just keep things to myself.*

+ + + + + + +

The next morning, I got up before the sun had risen and snuck out of the house with a few belongings in a satchel. I headed for the woods and tried hard to find my way back to the fighters' base. I failed. After two hours of wandering and knowing it shouldn't take that long, I gave up and headed for White Field. The forest was tranquil; only a few early birds decided to greet the morning with a little song. Other forest animals must have been scared of my presence and hidden. I came out of the dense forest into a clearing. The place seemed familiar. Maybe I was getting closer to the base. I ducked under some branches and then stepped up on a log. Hopping down from that, I avoided two holes in the ground and then stopped in a larger clearing to watch birds fly from one tree to another.

"Adrian Falkner." I whirled around, looking for the owner of the voice. "About time you showed up."

*Wait a minute! That voice belongs to the mysterious fighter.*

As soon as I had thought this, the fighter dropped silently from a tree in front of me.

"The name's Nahum," he said, holding out his hand. I shook it. Now that he wasn't covered in a cloak, I took a moment to look him up and down. His skin tone was a darker brown than mine, almost like caramel.

His brown hair curled slightly around his temples. In his left hand, Nahum carried a weapon unlike any I had seen before. Nahum was also observing me, his deep brown eyes glancing up and down like one who practiced noticing everything in seconds.

"Good to know who you are," I finally said, breaking the silence that had come over us. Nahum grinned.

"Don't be so sure of that. I'm more mysterious than you think," he said. "It's my job." Nahum jerked his head in the direction I had been heading. "Looking for The Enclave?" One of his thin eyebrows arched.

"Yeah, it turns out I'm not so great at that," I answered, feeling at ease with the guy. He chuckled.

"Actually, you weren't too far off," Nahum commented.

"What's with the name, by the way? I don't understand," I admitted.

"The Enclave? It's a portion of territory within or surrounded by a larger territory whose inhabitants are culturally distinct," Nahum replied. I blinked. He grinned. "In other words, The Enclave is the territory of our home where we are separated from the rest of Chahcan, and free to be Christ followers."

"Uh, that second definition only made a little more sense than the first," I said. Nahum chuckled.

"You'll get it eventually. Come on." Then, he began to lead the way. I followed at his side, watching as he switched his weapon between his hands several times.

"What's the weapon?" I asked as we walked. Nahum held it up so he could look more closely at it.

"It's called a Faze Whip. It's made with two joined shafts, held in place by a touch-sensitive latch. The handle in the middle is made of cedar and wrapped with leather. The curved blades at each end are unnoticeably different lengths, and face in opposing directions. This keeps the weapon at an angle so that it revolves naturally, making each swing smooth and powerful. The blades are made Damascus style with seration on the inside curve of the blade." Nahum pointed out each feature as he described them.

"Cool, but what's with the name? It's a double-sided spear, not a whip," I pointed out.

"When used in battle," Nahum said, brandishing his weapon as I stood a considerable distance from him, "the handle can stretch out." Gripping the bottom half of the handle, he swung the Faze Whip toward a tree. Remarkably, the middle of the handle disconnected, and the weapon reached another three feet up, hooking onto a limb above him. As the blade held firm to the branch, the handle sprang back together, taking Nahum up toward the tree. He flipped up the remaining distance and landed squarely on the limb. He jumped silently back down, watching my awestruck face.

"How does it do that?" I wondered.

"When I unhook the latch, it releases tension on a small metalic spring inside," Nahum explained, showing me. "This causes the shafts to launch apart from each other. A second spring then is activated, pulling the shafts back together. Then, I can lock the handle to prevent it from springing out again. It will always return to its original length."

"Neat."

"I can teach you how to use one if you want, then you can use it in the fight," Nahum said. There was something about him that I liked immediately, and we carried an easy conversation on the way to The Enclave. We had a much in common, I found out, even though he was two years older than me at eighteen. He was open in sharing information about the Defense's past.

They had been formed thirty-six years ago, making a pledge to protect the Chahcan natives. Ten years later, they arose to stop tyrrohns for the first time and won. However, the Ruling Heads were in opposition and sent forces to make the Defense disband. So, the Defense had gone into hiding and continued to fight the bigger enemies in secret.

"These tyrrohns are sent from the Ruling Heads as far as we know," Nahum continued. "Once the Ruling Heads found out that we were stronger in numbers, they've tried to find us. When that intelligence failed, I guess they went to more desperate measures." He shook his head and shrugged. "We can't be too quick to judge them, though."

We entered The Enclave, and Nahum led me to the same tent that Helyn had taken me to days earlier. Only one man was inside, Commander Naric, who was working on writing something.

"Well, look who the spy took hostage," Naric said, his voice a touch lighter than the time before. "Welcome back, Adrian." I nodded at him.

"He comes to help the fight, sir," Nahum said. I was thankful, momentarily, that I didn't have to inform the commander myself.

"You accept the quest?" Naric clarified, his eyes trained solely on me. To him, there seemed to be a difference between the fight and the quest. I had to open my mouth.

"Yes, sir," I answered. Naric clapped his hands together.

"Excellent. It's an answer to prayer. You'll start training immediately. Robert's already there waiting for something to do. Nahum, lead him to the Center and tell Robert of my order."

"Yes, sir," Nahum replied. Naric's response seemed very eager, and I began to wonder what I was getting myself into. Nahum pulled me farther into The Enclave and to a large clearing. The area, about fifty yards in both directions, was intentionally roped off, and formed a section off the back half of the southern side of The Enclave. There were about eighty to a hundred people already there, practicing using their bows, swords, spears, axes, and there were even some with Faze Whips. I couldn't get over how cool they looked and the way they worked. Some of the people were seated on the ground, deep in conversation. We found the leader, Robert, standing and watching the action which happened around him. Nahum explained Commander Naric's simple orders, and the man looked both proud and excited to have the opportunity.

"We begin immediately," he said eagerly. Nahum left to complete a mission but told me he'd check in later. "What weapons have you handled before?" Robert asked.

"I've shot a bow several times, and I remember using swords before," I answered. Truthfully, I hadn't shot a bow in at least six months, which was enough time to forget how to use one, and the only time I had handled a real sword was several years ago when I picked up one Dad had had on one of his trade ships. I hadn't actually used the weapon. Robert didn't hesitate, though, to put a sword in my hands. I quickly found myself, wooden sword in hand, listening to the instruction of Robert on how to hold my sword, what stance to take, and how to attack the sack-dummy in front of me.

"Good. Now attack! Blade up, Adrian! Block! Back up a bit more! Don't leave your middle exposed! Better! Now attack!" The instruction went on for an hour or so. Every time I even stepped wrong in a move, Robert quickly, and loudly, corrected me. At the end of the hour, though, I believed I had the footing figured out. Now it all came down to how to use the wooden sword. I was more than a little disappointed that I couldn't touch a real sword yet.

"Alright, Adrian, why don't you take a break? I'll be right back," Robert suggested, walking away. Everyone I knew had walked out of sight, so basically, I was alone for a few minutes. I ran my hand through my black, sweaty hair and sighed. I looked at the wooden sword-thing and threw it on the ground.

*This is entirely frustrating. Why can't I just hack into a few things with something real?* I wondered.

I walked over the sword-thing and went to a stump where cups of water sat. I took a sip and then, pouring the water into one hand, splashed it on my face. I looked over at the sack-dummy and instantly grew angry. I glared at the thing, squinting my blue eyes. I was tired of method and listening to instruction already. I simply wanted something that would inflict damage on that dummy.

"What happened to your sword?" Robert asked, surprising me from behind.

"I, uh, dropped it over there," I said carelessly.

"You dropped it?" he repeated. He mulled over these words. "Okay. I'm called away for the rest of the day, so feel free to pick up a bow or something. Just don't go crazy. Tomorrow, we'll practice different ways you can retrieve your sword if you've lost it. Should have started there in the first place." Robert again walked away, muttering instructions to himself. I shrugged, watching him leave. I looked at the young students who were shooting bows.

"Know how to use a bow?" I jumped, surprised to hear Helyn's voice. I whirled around to find her typical, teasing smile upon her face.

"Does everyone have to sneak up on me?" I asked.

"It's just fun with you. Your reactions are pretty good," Helyn replied.

"What reactions?"

"Like the time you ran into the tree, that was great." She was still teasing me.

*Okay, I'm a really easy target,* I thought.

"Do you know how to use a bow?" Helyn repeated.

"Yeah," I replied.

"Let's see how good you are," she challenged. A whole rack of bows sat in the area used explicitly for bow practice. At least ten targets sat a good thirty feet away, some further, supported by a short wood board. Helyn picked up an ornate bow, covered in corded leather and silver etchings.

"A reward I received from Robert," she mentioned. I examined the way she held it.

"Is that a left-handed bow?" I asked.

"Yup," she answered quickly and cheerfully. "What about you? Right or left-handed?"

"Left," I replied. She gave me an intrigued look and then handed me a left-handed bow that was not as ornate.

"You can use it for now. Maybe one day, you can get your own," Helyn said. She handed me arrows and then lined up at a target. I watched as Helyn quickly took aim and fired before I could analyze what she had done. All I saw was the arrow Helyn had shot, practically buried in the center of the target.

"Your turn," she told me.

*Aw, man, I'm going to make a fool of myself…again. No way am I going to hit the center first try.*

I aimed anyway, held longer than she did, and released the arrow. I looked for the arrow, expecting it to have hit way off the center, but to my surprise, it had lodged itself in the center just like Helyn's. Our targets looked like exact copies.

"Good shot," Helyn encouraged. I grinned. We shot for a while, and, in the beginning, I looked okay. The longer we shot, the more tired I got, and pretty soon, she was starting to make me look terrible. She had just fired, like, her twentieth perfect shot when I decided it was time to try something new.

"What other weapons do you fight with?" I asked her. She smiled and gave me a knowing look, but didn't mention it aloud.

"Axe mostly, but usually I'm not in close combat. Ever handled a sword?"

"Just did today, if you count the wooden-thing as a real sword," I answered, a little crossly. Helyn giggled.

"Robert's an enthusiastic teacher. He loves teaching the sword but be prepared! He's going to throw you some surprises," she advised.

"Thanks for the warning," I said. Helyn nodded, then she looked up.

"And time flies," she began. "It's already too late for you to go back to Copper Ridge."

"What do you mean? I know the way back in the dark," I defended.

"With the tyrrohns on you by now, you don't want to be out in the dark."

"Well, it's not like I can stay here," I protested. Helyn's brown eyes sparkled.

"Who says you couldn't?" Before I had time to comprehend everything fully, Helyn had pulled me to a tent in the middle of hundreds of others. How she knew this was the one she was looking for was a riddle to me. She called out and then from the tent came Nahum.

"Hello, Helyn." He eyed me with amusement, a smile on his lips.

"Good to see you again, and glad to have known where you were for once," Helyn replied. "Adrian needs to stay the night at The Enclave to avoid being captured by the tyrrohns. I was hoping you would be able to help me out." Nahum looked extremely eager to do anything for Helyn. Once Helyn had left to go to her accommodations, Nahum turned to me.

"And she continues to be one step ahead of you," he said.

"Oh, stop it," I objected. Nahum motioned me into the tent, and I stepped inside. Then, I saw what he meant. The place was already set up for two. Fur pallets were in the back of the tent, a good-sized rock served as a table, and two or three kerosene lamps lit the space.

"You live alone?" I inquired. Nahum sat down at the rock-table, setting his weapon down beside him.

"For the last two years, yes. My parents died in the fight against the last enemy." He sighed, then pointed to the food in front of him. "Let's eat." After the meal and some talking, sleep came quickly.

# CHAPTER FOUR

## A Morbid Curse

I walked swiftly for the Center, passing a bunch of people who I didn't know and who didn't know me. After a few minutes, I had to concede to asking one of the passing Defenders where it was, because I was completely lost. I reached the Center at the same time Robert did. Once again, giving me a wooden sword, his command was to drop it. He showed me two quick ways to get my sword back into my hand. He spent about thirty minutes showing me and letting me try in slow motion. Then, he stepped back.

"Okay, Adrian, pick up your sword!" he called to me. I grinned. By putting my foot quickly on the blade of the sword, then letting it slide off the blade, I made the handle raise and come to me. I grabbed it and quickly got into a fighting stance.

"Well done! Try the next one!" Robert called out. I dropped the sword, once again, onto the ground. I backed away from it a few steps. Then, I ran and, in one single motion, flipped onto the ground and came back up with the sword in hand. I rubbed a spot that had hit wrong. Robert walked up and chuckled.

"That one could use a little polishing. After the noon meal, Colin will come and teach you some agility skills that every fighter needs," he said. We got back to work. Another hour and a half of sword 'play' as Robert called it, which truly meant stance, attacks, and holding onto my sword as well as getting it off the ground if it fell. For a short time, he also grabbed a wooden sword and was my opponent.

The noon meal ended the sword lesson for the day. Robert left to help some Defenders with another duty, so I would have to eat alone. Thankfully, Robert had enough time to show me where the noon meal took place.

It was a long, narrow strip of cleared space between rows of tents. Down the center was a fire, built up in an oblong shape. About fifty women were gathered around the fire, stirring food in pots over the flames, pushing potatoes about in the ashes, or flipping grilled meat on large iron sheets. There was a considerable line at each of the twenty or more cooking stations, and I joined one. When I reached the end of the line, the woman serving me pointed toward the far end of the fire.

"There's water just at the end, drawn from the stream, and cups to drink from," she said. "If you like, you can sit close to the stream. The ground's soft." I didn't want to sit by the stream, but I was grateful to get a large cup of water. At last, I sat on the ground by myself, absentmindedly eating the food in front of me and drinking more than my share of water. I went for another sip after a bite of some exotic meat but found my cup empty. I'd have to get back in line. I sighed.

"Need another?" I looked up and found Commander Naric above me, holding out a cup of water. I took it from him.

"Thanks," I said, then took a big gulp.

"May I sit with you?" Naric asked. I nodded my consent, and he seated himself. "Is Robert working you hard?" I shrugged. "I wouldn't be surprised if he wasn't ever letting you take a break while he's present," Naric added as I took another gulp of water.

"He is pretty dedicated to the training," I admitted. "I haven't had a drink of water until now." There was a short silence as we finished our food and drinks. I took the time to look carefully at the leader. He was rather short, with dark brown hair and deep blue eyes. He was younger than his voice and duties made him look, maybe mid-twenties, but everything about him, his air, and his voice, made him become the part of a great leader.

"How long have you been one of the seven leaders?" I asked him. Naric turned his gaze entirely on me.

"Three years. I joined a short time after the core members went into hiding. Titus, another leader, is one of the core members. I was among those he talked to. He brought me to faith and joined me with the Defense."

"So, did he make you a leader immediately?"

"No, no, I had to earn it. For a while, I didn't think I would get the honor. Of course, I was young, only twenty-one. Moreover, Titus never went out of his way to make me known to anyone. I've since learned it was a wise decision on his part. Being a leader isn't anything about power. It's a huge responsibility, even with seven of us working. Training, meetings, plans, and missions. Sometimes I feel as though I'm needed everywhere at once."

Suddenly, someone called his name. "Speaking of being needed," Naric chuckled, rising from the ground. "So long, for now, Adrian. I look forward to having more time with you." I nodded. Naric nodded back and then was gone.

After taking one last drink, I went swiftly back to the Center, this time to meet Colin for agility training. I walked in view of the Center and unexpectedly caught sight of a familiar face.

"Alex?" I called. He spun around and gave me a confused look.

"What are you doing here, Adrian?" He was almost seething.

"I should be asking you that," I shot back.

"Well, there's this girl in town. You know, the one you didn't want to meet before. Her name is Helyn Thicket, but you probably haven't even noticed her. She keeps a lot of secrets, but I got her to tell me all about this place," Alex explained proudly.

"She'll speak to anyone who will promise not tell the location," I told him dryly, walking into the Center. Alex gave me an almost annoyed look.

"Sometimes, Adrian, your sarcasm is out of place," he criticized. I shrugged. "So, what are you doing here?" Alex asked.

"Training," I said, with minimal flare as we walked into the Center. "How long have you been here?"

"I just came today. Helyn had to get permission for me to come," Alex said.

*Yeah, I bet it was her pleasure.*

I reminded myself that girls were Alex's thing, and it sounded like Helyn had already been at Alex's place at least once. I found Colin among the crowd and, unintentionally, Helyn, who spotted us before Colin did.

"Hey, Adrian!" she called. "Hi, Alex," she added once we got closer. She didn't speak in any soft tone like other girls I had heard, just plainly. He nodded to her, going for cool and calm. I rolled my eyes.

"Well, Adrian, we meet again. Ready for some lively training?" Colin asked as jovial as ever.

"Sure," I answered. There was no way I was going to forget this leader. His smile and figure were unmistakable and his voice was memorable.

"Great. Okay, the first thing you need to know is that every work we do here is serious," Colin said, taking on a comical look that was a poor attempt to look serious.

I grinned and nodded, trying not to laugh. Helyn couldn't smother her giggle.

Colin continued, "Good. Now, we should test you and see your ability." He was playing with some daggers that he had on his belt. I eyed him skeptically.

"Um, I wouldn't start throwing daggers yet, Colin," I said. Colin let out a hearty laugh.

"No, most decidedly not. I would never throw daggers at you, not at any of even my most advanced students," he assured me. "We'll be using these." He somehow produced an oval-shaped ball. "It has just enough density to fly straight and far, but is soft enough that it won't hurt a person." He handed me the ball, and I instinctively gripped it like a Ledo ball.

"Although," Colin rubbed his chin musingly, "I might put these on the tips of an arrow once or twice, for the fun of it." He winked at me. "To start with, I'm going to stand over there, about twenty yards away, and you'll throw that at me. I'll dodge it, so you get the idea." He stepped the distance away and nodded for me to do so. I hesitated.

"You want him to throw that? At you?" Alex asked, suddenly coming alive. Knowing me, he could instinctively tell that I could throw this as I did one of my Ledo balls. However, I had my doubts about being able to hit Colin with it.

"Yes, that's what I said. Don't worry. I'll go easy on you," Colin confirmed. Alex started to protest, but then shrugged his shoulders and stepped back.

Colin stood still, ready to dive out of the way. I stood ready to throw, aimed, and flung the ball hard at him. Colin jumped to the right, my left, and I assume the ball was supposed to go right past him. Instead, it hit him in the chest, and he fumbled to hold on to it. Colin looked at me in surprise. I threw my hands in the air.

"Sorry, I didn't mean to show you up first try. I'm a Ledo player. I just made a lucky guess to which side you would jump," I explained.

"I tried to warn you," Alex added. Colin walked over, smiling, and no longer surprised.

"Ledo player. Okay, I can work with that." Then, he tried to turn serious again. "And remember," he added, "every work we do here is serious."

+++++++

Since Alex had now joined the Defense, Robert had decided that we should train together as a team. For two days, Alex and I were trained to work together, getting instructions on how to use swords, bows, and axes. Typically, I stuck with a sword, and Alex chose an axe. We dueled each other and fought Robert as a team. In those two days, I saw little of Helyn and only saw Nahum when he came back from work at night. On day three, Robert couldn't make it for training, but Helyn asked if we wouldn't mind a little friendly competition while we sharpened our bow skills.

So, Alex and I met her in the Center, and we grabbed our bows. We each had a target and a large handful of arrows to shoot.

At the start, everything went orderly, each of us taking turns and competing by keeping up with scores. We were the only ones shooting bows in the vast area. The closest person was at least seven yards away. By the end of round three, I had the highest score, which Alex claimed to be unbeatable. So, in round four, I felt good about my shot. I stood perfectly still, pulled back, and aimed. Just before I shot, though, something bumped me, and my fingers slipped. The arrow missed the target completely.

"What was that?" I asked. I looked at Alex, who grinned but shook his head. Helyn looked a little more smug as she gave me a sideways glance. "Oh, you want that kind of competition," I challenged.

"I have no idea what you are talking about," Helyn feigned innocence. Alex grabbed an arrow and aimed. Just before he shot, I snagged his bowstring with an arrow tip, and his arrow flew in a sort of wave. I couldn't help but laugh when the arrow didn't make it to the target.

"Hey!" Alex protested, but we ignored him.

"Bet you can't hit that target," Helyn contested, quickly pointing to a distant circle and readying her bow. I promptly got an arrow on the string, aimed and fired. Unfortunately, Helyn and I shot at the same time, and our arrows crossed paths stopping the other's flight. They both fell harmlessly to the ground a considerable distance away from the intended target. Meanwhile, Alex had readied his shot and got it off with just enough delay that it hit perfectly.

"Lucky shot," I taunted. "Try hitting that sack on the stump." Alex grinned.

"Okay," he agreed. I pulled back my bow with an arrow already nocked.

"Before me," I finished. Then, I let my arrow fly. Alex quickly let go of his, but mine made it there first, knocking the sack over. His arrow flew by and landed in the dirt beyond the stump.

"No fair," he complained. I tried to shoot the target I had missed because of Helyn's arrow, but before I let go, Alex shouldered me, and I fell off balance, landing in the dust. From behind me, Helyn laughed. So, I turned around and used my bow to trip her.

"Hey, I didn't do anything!" Helyn said as she fell over, her voice still hinting a laugh. Alex tried to make a comeback shot on his target for round four. He didn't miss it. Helyn and I stood up and fired arrows. Helyn went for her target, but I shot at Alex's. The arrow landed smack on the target's edge.

"What!?" Alex narrowed his eyes. Then, he aimed at my target and missed it.

"Nice shot," I teased. I'm not sure how, but we managed to move on to round five, and, thanks to some knocking about and false shots, I was falling behind the other two. Needless to say, their scores weren't much better. We shot at a bunch of other random items around that portion of the Center and the forestry beyond. Our arrows missed, flew high – and we never saw where they landed – they buried themselves in the dirt, and some hit the targets. Arrows were stuck everywhere.

Finally, we were all down to one arrow each. It was the end of the seventh round, I was the only one with an arrow left, and I needed to land this one in the center; otherwise, Helyn would win. I carefully aimed, held my breath, and then Alex pushed me from behind. I fell forward, releasing the arrow that landed a few feet in front of me. I dropped the bow and picked myself up.

"Really?!" I shouted, whirling on Alex.

"It's a basic rule," he said quietly, "you always let the girl win. Especially if she's as good with a bow as Helyn is." I shook my head. For the briefest minute, I was mad. Then, I looked at the mess we had made and burst out laughing. The other two quickly joined in. What had started as a little fun had turned into a competitive disaster. Arrows stuck out all over the place in seemingly random places, in trees, targets, and pretty much anything else that could have possibly been shot at. Despite losing, I realized that I had had fun.

"Oops. I didn't intend for this," Helyn said as the laughter died away.

"You had something more than good target practice in mind," I countered. Helyn shrugged, palms up, and raised her eyes heavenward. "Well, we'd better clean it up before Commander Naric sees it," I said, knowing he took the training seriously. We were about to run to gather the arrows we had shot when a voice came from behind us.

"I've already seen it." We froze at the sound of Commander Naric's disapproving voice. Helyn shot me a look and mouthed, oops. Instead of running to clean the mess, we turned around and faced the commander. "Competition can be healthy, or," he looked around, "it can be destructive." I wanted to argue that nothing had been destroyed, but decided quickly against it.

"Sorry." We all murmured in turn. Naric smiled.

"Considering the laughter, this competition was fairly healthy," he added. Helyn smiled.

"We'll clean it up," she offered. Commander Naric only shook his head and gave us something of a smile.

"No, it's not necessary." He raised a hand to keep us from protesting. "Despite the mess your bows caused, your accuracy is excellent. Yes, I was watching some of your competition. I've been told how well you all have been progressing in your training over the last few days, and I think it's time you are sent on your first mission. A test. As a team." I was pleased that he included Helyn in his address.

"What are we doing?" Helyn asked.

"I want you three to go and search the Underground."

"Underground?" I asked.

"Yeah, Adrian, a place under the ground," Alex told me, in a smart-aleck tone. Helyn gave him an incredulous look.

"Sarcasm isn't your thing, is it?" she inquired of Alex. Before the shock of the question could wear off, Helyn continued, "Adrian, it's a series of tunnels that cover the whole of Copper Ridge, White Field, and they even stretch into the twin towns, Veaus and Vainus. They were made back during the Wars of Old. The tunnels were used to get inside the enemies' camps secretly."

"And what are we searching for in the Underground?" I queried. Naric answered this time.

"Signs of our enemy. There was once a time when he had a command center there. We're pretty sure he's moved to a new area, but anything he might have left behind that seems of worth you can bring back."

"How do we get there?" Alex inquired.

"Portals." For a moment, I didn't move wondering if he'd explain. He didn't. "Come on. I'll show you the entrance. Gather your weapons," Naric ordered.

We hurriedly gathered our weapons. I grabbed a sword instead of a bow because my fingers hurt from pulling back the string. We trekked in silence, following Naric's lead, for about fifteen minutes, taking a straight course away from the southern border of The Enclave. Finally, we reached the spot. On the ground, mostly covered by leaves and fallen branches, was a metal plate. We worked as instructed to remove the branches. Naric reached down and pulled the plate up from the ground; it swung open like a door.

"They're called portals. They're doors to the Underground. There are hundreds over the tunnels," Naric explained. Helyn went down first, taking the crude stairs on the wall that led to the tunnels below. I went second. Alex came after me. I stopped momentarily to look up as the portal door fell shut above us. That was it. No final instructions from Naric. We were officially on our first mission. Alex's foot came down and kicked me.

"Hey! I'm down here," I protested.

"Keep moving, will you?" Alex growled.

"I'm moving."

"Well, you're really slow."

"I'm down already."

"You weren't a minute ago!"

"Just get down here," I shouted up. Alex dropped to the ground, straightened his shirt, and huffed. The look he gave me was almost a glare. At the same time, we both turned to look at Helyn, as if we had suddenly remembered she was with us. She gave us an amused look, then led the way into the Underground. Just as the Wars of Old, the Underground was like a relic from centuries ago. The walls consisted of packed and compressed dirt that fell every now and then. Eventually, I took the lead through the tunnels, and we scoured the empty place. About an hour later, we had seen only an occasional sign of anyone else having even walked through the tunnels before us.

"There's not much down here," Helyn observed, being very generous with her words.

"Just a lot of dirt," Alex added, as a fresh pile dumped on his head. Alex rubbed his hair, shaking the dirt out.

"Looks good. Need more?" Grinning, I bumped the wall, and more fell on his head.

"Hey!" he protested, shaking his head while Helyn and I laughed. "Thanks," he said insincerely.

"Anytime. Let's go," I suggested. The others agreed, and we turned around to find a portal. Suddenly, I had no idea where to go. I had often gone places without knowing how I had gotten there, but there had always been the sun to get me back. Now all I could see were endless empty tunnels.

"No one, by any chance, happens to know which way we came, do they?" I asked with little hope.

"Oh great, you got us lost," Alex complained. I looked at Helyn.

"You've been down here before, haven't you?" To my dismay, she shook her head.

"No, I've only seen the maps," she answered, somewhat sympathetically. I decided that I would just go with my instinct.

"Okay, we're going that way," I said, pointing to the path behind us. Helyn came quickly to follow my lead.

"Why that way?" Alex questioned skeptically.

"Any better ideas?" Helyn asked. Alex considered the privilege of answering the question for a minute. Then, he shook his head. "Then, we follow Adrian," Helyn said with finality. It felt strange to have Helyn so abruptly rely on me to lead. I wondered if that was Naric's plan all along. We began walking, taking paths without hesitation. At one fork, Helyn suggested left, and I went with it. After another half hour or so, though, Alex began to criticize my ability to navigate labyrinths.

"Are you sure you know where you're going?"

"No," I answered.

"Maybe we should go back to that last turn and go the other way."

"We aren't turning around and backtracking progress," Helyn argued.

"I thought Naric said there were hundreds of these portals," Alex pointed out. "Why haven't we run into another by now?"

"Do you always focus on the negative?" Helyn wondered. Alex frowned.

"Typically, I'm optimistic. It's just this setting is perfect for..." he hesitated.

"Ghosts?" I guessed, turning to give him a critical look. Helyn laughed at the idea.

"You don't have anything to worry about," she assured him.

"Oh, so your enemy didn't used to house his weapons and soldiers down here? It's not possible he'll return?" Alex spouted.

"Wow," I exclaimed. "And your sarcasm just got better."

"Our enemy isn't a ghost, Alex," Helyn added.

"Are you two just teaming against me on purpose?" Alex posed. Helyn and I exchanged glances.

"Sorry," Helyn offered. "You did bring up the ghosts."

"And it is an impossible idea," I asserted. Alex stuck his hands in his pockets and fell silent. Up ahead, I spotted an unusual, orange light in the tunnel. Hopeful, I ran forward, looking up. Sure enough, there was the portal.

"It's about time," I muttered. We let Helyn climb up first, and Alex went next. I was halfway up my climb when something grabbed my foot. I gave a quick shout as I slipped a step or two down the ladder.

"Adrian, come on!" Alex called. Holding on tighter with my hands, I looked down at my foot. I unexpectedly met the bright gaze of a dark figure that held onto me. Startled, my hands released their grip. Then, I was falling toward the horrible figure.

"Aahhhh!" I screamed, falling on top of the ghostly figure. As soon as I landed, I rolled away and stood up, drawing my weapon. The eyes never left me, staring me down with their pulsing light. I stood a reasonable distance from him as he stood.

"What are you going to do with that, boy?" the figure asked. The voice sent a chill up my spine. It was a voice to match the appearance; almost a whisper that made the words sound cold. The sound seemed to be unreal as if the figure in front of me wasn't alive. I reminded myself that ghosts were real. The bright eyes, which were like an ice blue, stared at the sword I held.

"Do you plan to fight me while I am yet unarmed?" the whispery voice spoke once again.

"Maybe," I said, my voice surprisingly steady. "Maybe not. Depends on what threat you bring."

"Threat? To you?" the voice seemed to be confused. "I bring no threat. I only bring a calling."

"You could have chosen a better way to bring it," I said, still very wary of the figure. The eerie figure let out a raspy chuckle.

"What do you have to say?" I asked, cutting the horrible noise short.

"I bring the calling to be who you really are," came the reply.

"What are you talking about?"

"Come on, stop playing the false part of a fool! Don't you remember your past?" the figure posed.

"What do you know of it?" I demanded. He let out another chuckle. A sudden dread washed over me, a cold sensation like the one that had coursed through my hands after I touched the tyrrohn leader.

"Who are you?" I challenged boldly.

The figure didn't move or answer. "What do you have to do with the Defense?" The eyes that had been unblinking and trained on me fell momentarily. At that exact moment, Alex and Helyn dropped down the ladder within seconds of each other. Alex flung his axe at the figure, who dodged it. The pulsing gaze of the figure was focused on them now. That alone was enough to move the two at a safer distance behind the figure, directly across from me. The lantern in Alex's hand shone on the figure, giving his body an eerie glow. The eyes once more locked on me.

"Will you answer the calling?" the whisper persisted. I narrowed my eyes in a challenge.

"Only when you answer me: who are you?" I bargained.

With slight hesitation, the answer came: "Death." The tone that the whisper took on was strange, almost regretful, yet it carried some leisure. For one moment, I couldn't respond, and all the courage flew from me. Again, the cold sensation crept over my body, draining away my strength. I gripped my sword tighter, frowning in the concentration it took. I raised the sword.

"You can give my answer to whoever has sent you," I said. "No!" I ran and swung the sword at him. To my surprise, Death only raised his arms to defend himself, crossing them in front of his body. My sword collided with his arms and stopped in its tracks. It inflicted no wound. I had no time to consider what had happened because Death then threw me backward. The unusual feeling left me as I got back up and raised my sword to block an intended hit. From behind Death, Helyn raised her bow, aimed, and shot an arrow at him. He dropped, taking me down with him. I pushed him off me and stood as quickly as possible.

"Go, go, go," I told Helyn and Alex, motioning swiftly to the ladder. They ran for it, climbing as fast as they could.

"Are you so determined to rid yourself of the past?" Death's voice came as I ran for the ladder myself. "Why fight what is to be? Own up! You don't belong with the Defense!" I was once again halfway up the ladder, Alex had taken my sword, and Death grabbed onto to me. I held tight and tried to shake him off.

"Adrian!" I looked up and accepted the arrow Helyn offered. I turned it tip down and thrust it again and again at Death's face. Strangely enough, it hurt him. He released his grip, and I jumped up the last few stairs. Alex slammed the portal door shut, and we took off, racing away from the Underground.

"What did I tell you?" Alex shouted. "It was a perfect setting for ghosts!"

# CHAPTER FIVE

## One Last Breath

Edmund Naric knew of our arrival the moment we set foot in The Enclave and met us with a barrage of questions. We described what we had seen, rather awkwardly going through getting lost and having to wander till we had found an exit. Alex tried his best to paint himself in a good light but failed miserably. Then came the mysterious part. I explained the sudden appearance of the figure, falling back down with him and parts of the conversation that had come before Helyn and Alex joined me in the Underground. Alex insisted on his 'ghost story'. Helyn didn't step in to describe the figure; instead, she hurried to tell of his introduction. Though the name didn't ring a bell with the leader, he knew as much as I did: Death was our enemy.

"It was weird," Alex said after we had finished the basic story. "Death totally ignored Helyn and me and went straight to Adrian. He never said a word to either of us."

"He didn't have to," Helyn pointed out. "He never had to say anything to push us away and go after Adrian again."

"But what did he want with Adrian?" Naric questioned. All eyes turned to me, and I shrugged like I didn't know. As if Death's words hadn't made me want to vomit. Naric continued, glancing up at the sky, "You two will probably have to spend the night here again. I hope your parents won't be concerned." His eyes glanced between Alex and me.

"My parents are cool with it," Alex answered simply. "They know I'm with Adrian."

"Mine don't mind," I said.

"Well, alright. Helyn can take you back to your tents, if you need a little guidance," Naric hinted. Helyn flashed a teasing smile as the commander left.

"Yeah, you two definitely need help," she quipped. "I'm glad your parents are good with letting you stay. You wouldn't want to get caught in the dark on the way back to Copper Ridge right now," she added. I immediately had an image of what I had seen last time I had traveled the roads of Copper Ridge in the dark. Something clicked, but I clamped my mouth shut for the moment.

"What about you, Helyn?" Alex asked.

"I'm staying in The Enclave, too. I do so many times in the week," she replied. Helyn led Alex and me to the tent where Alex was staying. I told her I could find my way to Nahum's tent. Helyn agreed and then disappeared.

"Alex, that figure in the Underground," I began, now that Helyn was gone.

"What of it?" Alex wondered, almost disgustedly.

"He's the same one I saw on the streets that night. You know, I told you about it," I answered.

"Great! Adrian has a ghost figure haunting him," Alex exclaimed.

"Not a ghost," I insisted. "Though I wonder…why he didn't disappear when the light hit him this time?"

"Maybe my parents' lantern, the one I left behind in my room, is magical. Maybe…"

"Just stop right there." I held up my hand. Alex could take things a little too far…most of the time. Nonetheless, it wasn't a welcome confirmation that this figure seemed to be stalking me. The Defense leaders had been right to say their enemy was targeting me. I left Alex and found Nahum's tent. He hadn't come back yet. I was tired, but sleep was not the first thing on my mind. Death's words came alive in the darkened tent and seemed to echo inside my head. I couldn't help but see the truth in his words. His calling 'to be who you really are' ran through my mind, followed by the horrible question, 'don't you remember your past?' I fought and fumed against the unfairness of the statements. My past was Morro's doing. I wanted to fight the tyrrohns, not be their ally. It wasn't my fault they killed Ruling Heads with the weapons I gave Morro. Finally, I shook my head to rid the thoughts and lay on the cot. For a long time, I tossed and turned. However, sleep eventually came.

+++++++

Morning dawned brightly and was a welcome change from the dark in Nahum's tent. I went straight to the Center, but as I looked around, no one I knew was in sight. I figured Alex would be sleeping in. The leaders, I assumed, must be busy. Nahum had not come back, to my knowledge, last night. So, I was alone. I took off to wander throughout The Enclave, watching different goings-on. I came to a section I hadn't ever seen before, where an uncountable number of horses were grazing. I gaped at the sight and wondered why I hadn't seen it before.

"Pretty, aren't they?" Helyn asked cheerfully, coming up behind me.

"How in the Fallen Lands do you keep them hidden?"

"Oh, they don't all stay here. Some of them are my father's."

"Your father's? Is he involved with the Defense?" I inquired, glancing around as if he might be close by. Helyn shook her head.

"No, but he technically gave the horses to me for my use. Others in White Field have done the same thing. They bring the horses whenever Commander Naric thinks we might have to move."

"So, we might be moving?" I frowned. Helyn shrugged.

"I don't get told such things," she replied. Her smile disappeared. "The things I do get told are enough to handle."

"What do you mean?" I turned my attention entirely away from the horses. Helyn frowned.

"Well, okay. So, I can safely live in White Field, and trade, and do all those other things that 'normal' people do. As a result, Naric has commissioned me to help the others who live in White Field to bring in supplies for the Defense." She halted.

"And there's a problem?" I guessed.

"Yup." Helyn regained her joyful manner. "Money has always been a problem within the Defense."

"Oh, yeah, I can't see why," I put in sarcastically. Helyn laughed.

"I'm just wasting my time worrying. The Lord will provide. He always has. I have to head back to White Field. My parents will be looking for my return. See you later, Adrian Falkner." Helyn slipped among the herd of horses, somehow picked out one of hers, and rode away. The minute she disappeared, I set my jaw with determination. A thought had entered my head, and it didn't seem unreasonably wrong.

*Maybe Death is right. I should be who I am. You're a thief, Adrian. Now, the Defense needs supplies, and who would be better than you to slip into Copper Ridge and make quick work of it? They won't care where it came from. It'll be a couple nights' work, but you've stolen five nights a week before,* I told myself.

"I'll do it," I muttered, nodding.

+++++++

Right at sunset that night, I crept into Copper Ridge and headed for the Market. I had things all figured out in my head. There were at least three different stores that I could hit in one fell swoop. The Market was the easiest. Knowing the owner, I knew that the backdoor was never locked, and, better yet, he often forgot to close the front window. The fact had never mattered to me before, but I was grateful now for the knowledge. I got to the Market and ducked into the alley beside it. After waiting in the dark for several minutes and hearing nothing, I decided to see if anyone was inside the building. Sneaking to the front, I saw the light in the open window, and voices suddenly began.

"I haven't seen Adrian for a while," the shop owner said in his characteristic drawl. His words froze me. Who was he talking to? I crouched within hearing range, but out of sight.

"That's true." It was Mom's voice undoubtedly. Yet, there was something different about it.

"Been getting himself into trouble lately?"

"I wouldn't know." Mom's voice fairly shook, with what emotion, I didn't know.

"Well, uh, good-night to you," the shop owner said hesitantly. I raced around the side of the building again and watched Mom leave. I waited until I heard the door close and saw the shop owner disappear down the street. Quick as lightning, I was through the open window and inside the Market. I looked around, trying to assess what I should grab first. As I moved to grab a jar off the shelf, something made my arm feel suddenly heavy. A deep-set dread washed over me, and my whole body was shaking. Morro came to mind immediately, and I halted.

"It's not like when Morro told you to steal. This is right," I spoke. "The Defense needs supplies. People could die without this." Once again, my arm went toward the food and I pulled it back. Was it right? All I could think at that moment was, Morro would be pleased. I clenched my fists.

"I don't want to please Morro. I hate him and hate who he made me," I muttered vehemently. Death's calling rang in my ears. "I'm not who Morro made me! It's been six long years. I'm not like that anymore." Suddenly, what I was doing hit me in the face—stealing again. The reality had never had so much weight before. I shook my head.

"No. Not for Morro, not for me, not for the Defense. Not for anyone!" My voice level was rising. Before I could give it a second thought, I whirled around and left the building. I raced through the streets and back into the woods. Somehow, I found my way back to The Enclave and even Nahum's tent. Nahum wasn't in. I collapsed on the bed, breathing hard from the run. It was only then that I had second thoughts.

*Maybe I should have done it. After all, Helyn did say they needed supplies. Yet, she didn't say they were desperate.* I huffed at my indecision.

"The Lord will provide," Helyn had also said.
"Well, I sure hope she's right."

+ + + + + + +

I woke up the next morning, hot with anger. I went to the Center and found Robert waiting for training, but I couldn't focus and found myself glad when he was called away. Alex hadn't shown, but I had no excuse for what could be keeping him. That is until I saw him and Helyn coming toward me.

"Did you hear?" Helyn called out. I shook my head. "The Lord provided!" I stared at her like she had gone mad.

"Uh, provided what?" Alex asked.

"The needed supplies for the Defense. Colin came to tell me this morning when I rode in. A Defender from White Field came during the night to give Naric money he had been saving up for a time. I'm heading to town right now. Didn't I tell you the Lord would provide?" Helyn left me with a beaming smile, and I stared at her quizzically.

"Do you know what she's talking about?" Alex asked me. I shrugged.

"Sort of."

"What does she mean, 'the Lord provided'?" he questioned. Again, I shrugged.

"I heard that a Defender provided. I didn't see her lord do anything," I retorted. Still, a weight felt like it had slipped from my shoulders. At least the Defenders were no longer in need.

+++++++

The next morning, I went to the Center, where Alex, Robert, and Naric were waiting for me. Instead of waiting to hand me a weapon, Robert was waiting for me to join their group on the ground, which I did.

"We thought that we would spend some time with Naric, while he had the time, to talk about the foundation of the Defense," Robert explained.

Naric started, "The Defenders have always had two goals. The first is to stop any attacks against the people of Chahcan or against us. When tyrrohns threatened to kill, the Defenders stepped up to stop them. They succeeded in that mission. But our second goal is higher and greater: to give God the glory for all things. You've been told that the Ruling Heads opposed our efforts and sent men to force us to disband? Well, it wasn't because of our fighting efforts. It was because of Whom we were claiming gave us victory. Many people oppose our beliefs and, therefore, don't appreciate our actions."

"What are your beliefs?" I asked skeptically.

"I was hoping you'd be willing to listen. Have you heard about the Christian faith?"

"Um, some," I mumbled. Alex and I exchanged glances. Bridge's lectures on religions and superstitions flashed across my mind.

"Then, perhaps it is best to start at the beginning." Naric opened a book that he had with him. "You've heard of the Bible?"

"Yes," Alex answered for us. We had heard what it was and what it represented, once again, from Bridge. I had a feeling I knew where this was heading.

"The first book of the Bible is Genesis. It means beginning. Genesis records the beginning of the world. In the first two chapters, we read that God created the world just by speaking it into existence in just six days."

"Six days?" Alex exclaimed.

"Day one, God created light. He separated the light from the darkness, making day and night. Day two, He separated the sky from the seas. Day three, He created dry land and all the vegetation. Day four, the sun, moon, and stars. Day five, flying creatures and creatures that lived in the seas. On day six, God created all land creatures. Then, He created man in His own image. 'Male and female, He created them.' He put them in His garden and gave them dominion over all the animals. All His creation was good, very good. There was no death, no corruption. Everything was perfect." Naric was quoting everything from memory, looking at Alex and me instead of the book in his hands.

"The foundation of what we believe is that God is the Creator. He formed this earth," Robert stated. Then, he added, "From the first eleven chapters of Genesis, we can learn all about the origin of sin, the punishment for sin and its effect on our world, of the world-wide flood that changed the world, and of different languages."

"Great. So, after the creation, what happened? Obviously, the world isn't perfect," Alex fired up. For the first time in a while, I wholeheartedly agreed with Alex's outburst.

"Genesis three," Naric sighed. "The first man and woman that God created rebelled against God's only rule. Do not eat the fruit from the Tree of the Knowledge of Good and Evil. Eve, the first woman, was deceived by a serpent, but Adam, the first man, sinned with his eyes wide open. From his disobedience comes our corrupted world, which is filled with sin. Yet, even back then, God promised to send One to bring salvation. Before the fall of man, Adam and Eve could walk with God in the garden He had created for them. Afterward, they had to be thrown out of the garden and separated from God. Since that time, we have all been born with a sinful nature that separates us from God."

"Wait, what sin?" Alex asked.

*Only perfect kids like Alex can ask that question*, I thought.

I had heard about sin and God's wrath against it before. It wasn't exactly something I wanted to delve into again. I had tried to leave that stuff in the past.

Naric answered Alex's question calmly. "Sin is rebellion against God and His will for us. God has set up many rules that all of us have defied." Alex gave Naric an amused look but remained silent.

"Helyn and I had a short talk about this, sort of," I said. "Referring to the passage in Fighters from Ancient Days that talked about our death."

"And what did you determine?" Naric asked eagerly.

"That we haven't truly died, but that, figuratively, we were already dead because we couldn't make things right with God," I answered. I deemed it easier to stay on the 'I'm already dead' side of the conversation, rather than go further. I hoped my statements would keep Naric and Robert going in that direction.

"Exactly," Naric agreed. "Instead of figuratively, maybe spiritually would be a better word for understanding this. I'm glad you've read the book ahead of this time. This is what we come to realize, sooner or later: that we are sinners, that the penalty for our sin is death and we need salvation."

*And he just took it farther,* I sighed.

I pulled up some of the grass by my feet and began twisting it around my fingers. Robert picked up the telling, "Now comes the amazing part, the fulfillment of God's promise to save us. God sent His one and only Son to come and die for us, to take our punishment. His Son was born of a virgin; He was both God and man in one."

Their statements were confusing me and I wanted to walk away, but their enthusiasm held me. Maybe I just wanted to hear how the story ended. Naric explained, with Robert jumping in every now and then, how God's Son, Jesus, had walked the earth and taught the people. While some of the people believed, especially His close followers, most did not see Him as the Son of God come to save them. Some even hated Him so much that they plotted to kill Him, with the help of the Romans, whom they despised.

"They crucified our Lord," Naric said reverently. "Jesus died and took our punishment, satisfying God's wrath. Then, He was buried in a tomb. Three days after His death, Jesus Christ rose from the dead."

"Wait a minute. The guy you believe in is a ghost?" Alex cut in. Robert snorted, and Naric shook his head. I wanted to laugh, but Naric was already talking.

"Absolutely not! After His resurrection, Jesus appeared to over five hundred people, proving that He is indeed living and the Son of God. Now, through belief in Jesus Christ and confession of our sins, we can have a right standing with God." There was a long moment of silence between us after Naric had finished. I was trying to reconcile the thought of an angry God offering us life. It didn't make sense.

"Well?" a new voice broke the silence. I jumped and jerked my head around to find that, once again, Helyn had snuck up behind me.

*I've got to start figuring out when she's going to appear and stop making myself look bad,* I determined.

"Does that start to answer your question about how we save ourselves from dying?" Helyn asked. I shrugged.

"Maybe a little," I said noncommittally.

"Good," Helyn smiled. Robert and Naric rose from their places on the ground.

"Well, I think that's enough for a time," Robert said. "If you have any questions, though, either of us would be happy to answer them." Both the leaders walked away, leaving Alex, Helyn, and me in the Center. Helyn went off to practice with her axe, and Alex, not-so-stealthily, followed her. I wanted to do something to get my mind off of the lesson.

"How about some training?" I grinned as I turned to face Nahum, who was brandishing his Faze Whip. In his right hand, he held an idle Faze Whip. He tossed it my way. I caught it and looked over the features.

"Come on. We'll head into the woods and see about scaling some trees. I heard you've been training with Colin, how's that been?" Nahum asked. I told him about the first day and how I had hit Colin with the ball. He laughed.

"That Colin, he's going to get himself into trouble one day. Of course, we all are going to get ourselves in trouble with the Ruling Heads one day so…" Nahum shrugged. "These trees will work." Nahum showed me how to latch and unlatch the lock on the handle, and had me practice it. Then, he taught me how to 'throw' the blade out toward an opponent like a whip. After that, Nahum challenged me to 'fight' him. I took up the challenge, and we 'fought.' The whole time he gave me tips and techniques on how to handle the blade. After the lesson, as we talked it over in his tent, I quickly decided that the Faze Whip was the weapon I enjoyed using the most.

# CHAPTER SIX

## A Spiritless Cold

The next morning, I found myself waiting around in the Center for someone I knew to show up. I had been at The Enclave a week and a half, and Robert had always been waiting for me. I wandered in circles watching others come and start training with other leaders, or even by themselves, picking up their weapons and beginning well-known drills. Among the leaders I didn't know a one, Colin didn't even come. After a while, just before I could decide to leave the Center, I heard an almost familiar voice.

"Have time to talk?" Commander Naric asked on approach.

"I'm not doing anything else," I answered. Jerking his head in a direction, Naric started to walk away, and I followed at his side.

"Robert and Colin are occupied with a matter concerning the Defense. Anyway, I talk better when I walk. I have space to think," Naric explained.

"Funny, when I walk, I tend not to think," I thought aloud. Naric smirked.

"I'll try not to walk too slowly," he jested. "You seemed, at least, mildly interested in my story. I thought that while I had time, I would share it with you. Maybe it will inspire you." I gave him the go-ahead. "I was a kid full of dreams and plans. I always told myself that I would single-handedly defeat the enemies that Chahcan had made. I guess I had aspired to be a hero," Naric grinned at me. "It was never to be, I knew it even at ten, but I continued to let myself dream. After all, what harm was there in dreaming?"

"Can't say I've ever had an inspiration like that," I interjected.

"Well, some of us do, and some of us don't. My father was in Chahcan's militia. He used to teach me different parts of what he was learning when he came home. Eventually, my dreams of liberating Chahcan included my father. He was as good as any man could be, he was brave and kind, and I had figured all the stuff he could do might come in handy. My father was called into war when I turned twenty. Thirty days later, he was missing in action. I became a broken young man on the day my father couldn't be found.

"Then, everyone started talking about the Defense. The words on everyone's lips were things like 'the Defense did this' or 'the Defense said that.' I followed these people around secretly, interested in what they were doing, not so much what they were saying. They were doing what I had aspired to do myself. At the time, I was kind of furious at them for doing what my father and I should have been doing. I watched as they succeeded in their fight against those set on destroying Copper Ridge and White Field. I was among the crowd when they gave their speech after the battle was won. It was there that Titus found me."

"He's the one who brought you into the Defense," I remembered.

"Yes. Titus spoke with me about their message and their mission, and I became more than interested. We became friends and conversed daily about the Lord and their purpose. Soon after I turned twenty-one, I gave my life to the Lord. Then, the Defense was opposed by the Ruling Heads, and they went into hiding. Shortly afterward, a miracle came into my life. After an entire year, my father was found." Naric paused, taking a deep breath.

After a moment, Naric went on, "he was injured and never really the same after the whole experience, but it didn't matter. He had come back. I told my father about the Defense, and he suggested that we let passing Defenders be allowed to take refuge in our home. I was thrilled with the idea. My mother and father stayed at their home, but I joined the Defense as they went into hiding. I spent two more years training, learning the Scriptures, and teaching others who came. For a while, we grew daily. Then, the numbers became steady; we neither increased nor decreased in number. Thus, we have stayed for a long time. Two and a half years after I had come into the Defense, they called me to be a leader. Of course, you know I accepted and have all the duties that come with that."

"That's…great," I said when it seemed like he was waiting for me to speak. Naric smiled.

"You're wondering what this has to do with you, right? Why would I give so much detail about my personal life? Well…I'm going to be honest, Adrian, from the first time I met you, I was struck with a resemblance between you and myself."

"I remind you of yourself?"

"Sounds kind of conceited, doesn't it?" Naric chuckled. "More specifically, you remind me of myself before Christ changed me. May I ask you a question?"

"Uh, sure."

"Yesterday, when Robert and I were sharing the Gospel with you, I sensed you were averse to it. Will you tell me why?" His blue eyes were piercing. I looked away.

"I just…I mean, it's not like I hadn't heard that stuff…before," was my stammered reply.

"I see," Naric nodded. "My spiritual story goes much deeper than it appears. My family and I had known of the faith for a while, I knew some scripture, I even knew the story of Christ, but I never truly took any of it to heart. When my father went missing, I grew angry at the God I was told controlled the earth. When Titus found me, it quickly became apparent to him that I was seeing God all wrong. What I needed to see and hear of Him was His goodness, His love, His grace, and His mercy."

"Are we still talking about me?" I wondered.

"I'll just say this," Naric began. "This quest that you've accepted is one of the greatest things you will undertake, but there is a humbleness involved."

"What do you mean?" I asked although I was hoping this conversation as close to its end.

"You have to be willing to change. Change can be a good thing. Without change, you will never achieve your goal. Pride cannot be allowed to become a stronghold." Naric stopped walking and turned to face me, looking me straight in the eye. "We can't always win," he said. "And, sometimes, the win we do gain does not always seem to have the effect we wanted." Naric turned and continued walking. I followed reluctantly, and my gaze wandered to a group of teenagers – Nahum among them – standing in a group, all holding weapons; they seemed ready to leave. Naric followed my gaze.

"They are spies, an elite group that is heading out for another mission of gathering information," he said.

"They're going to Death's place to gather information?" I asked, a little surprised.

"Sometimes they have done so, but this time, no." I wanted to know more, but I didn't feel it was my place to inquire.

The group raised their weapons and shouted, "For the Prophecy and the Promise of Christ!" Then, they quickly filed out to begin their mission. I turned back to Naric.

"What was that?" I asked him.

"It's the Defense's mantra," Naric said, his shoulders straightening. "The Promise of Christ has two meanings. One: that He will redeem us. Two: that He will come again. And when He does, we shall be taken to Heaven and live with our Lord." He seemed inspired by repeating the words.

"What about the first part?"

"The Defenders have always followed a prophecy, some written code on which they base their battles. We choose our battles wisely, Adrian, we don't just fight anyone who unnerves us." Naric paused. "I should add that the prophecies we follow have been written down by men before us who were inspired by the Lord."

"What prophecy do you follow now?" I inquired. Naric seemed to stall on this question. For a moment, I thought he didn't know.

"Adrian, I don't mean to offend you, but the prophecy is to be known among certain Defenders only. I don't have the freedom to share it with you," he answered.

"Oh." Though he meant not to offend me, I still took it personally. I wasn't trusted.

"You don't have to be angry at me. I have faith in you. I'm just under a code. I have to take orders too." He stopped walking and turned to me. "I have no doubt you will fulfill your duty."

"How can I know?"

"Trust. Believe that the Lord has called you and will see you through the end. Even if it's not everything that you think it will be, and even if you change to become another man." Naric looked me square in the eye. "You must know who you are and by what means you stand." From a pocket, he produced a chain. Hanging from it was a wooden cross. He held it out to me. I felt obliged to take it.

"It will always bring you back to where you need to be," Naric said. I pulled the chain over my head and let the cross settle on my chest. For some reason, I felt like he wasn't saying that it was a portal that could transport me places, even though that was the first thing that crossed my mind. I felt that it meant something I couldn't understand.

"Could I ask you one more thing?" I asked, my mind wandering from the subject a little. I heard Naric's name called. Naric ignored it and nodded. "Why exactly is there death?"

"Why do we have to die and others around us? It's because of sin, Adrian. Robert and I told you about the fall of man, how we disobeyed God. Well, believe it or not, there was no sin in the world until after that point. Only after Adam sinned did death enter the world...and with it, death." I nodded and didn't look at him.

*I had a feeling he would say that.*

"Christ defeated death," Naric continued boldly, bringing my gaze back to his face. "By dying on the cross and then rising again, He defeated the sting of death. As it says in the Bible, 'Where, O death, is thy victory? Where, O death, is thy sting?' Christ took it away for those who believe in Him because they will live forever in heaven with Him after death."

*I don't understand*, I thought, straining to keep from speaking my thoughts aloud. *That doesn't make any sense.*

+ + + + + + +

I sat in the Center after training as the evening faded, fingering the hilt of my sword. Robert had given me a real sword to work with, one forged by a Defender in another part of The Enclave. It was mine, he said, so long as I promised I wouldn't get frustrated and toss it across the woods. I guess he knew me better than I thought he did.

"Hey, whatcha doing?" Helyn asked, her cheery voice matching her big smile. She sat down beside me, leaning against the tree behind us.

"Thinking," I replied.

"Funny, I thought you didn't like to think," she teased me. I shrugged. "What are you thinking about?" she asked, her teasing tone coming down a notch. Thoughts from previous days came in like a flood, and I frowned, trying to pick one to tell her. Unfortunately, Morro was at the front of my mind.

"Um, I'm thinking about Morro," I answered slowly.

"Who is he?" Helyn asked.

"A traitor." Helyn leaned forward as if eager to hear an exciting story. I sighed. "He was my older brother and, for a time, my role model. I copied everything he did, followed in his footsteps, even…even to the point of stealing for him. If Morro asked for it, I did my best to get it. Little did I know that he was handing everything over to a group of tyrrohns. Then, one night, we got caught in the act. Morro left me and made his way safely out of town. I got caught and left with the record of a thief and…tyrrohn ally." My voice had taken on an edge.

"You're angry at him," Helyn said, very softly.

"Don't I have a right to be?" I fired up.

"You have a right to be hurt, yes," Helyn answered. I frowned deeper; it wasn't a direct answer to my question. She leaned back against the tree again. We were silent for a while.

"I don't really know what to say or how to help you," Helyn admitted. "But I know the One who does. You only have to talk to Him; He'll listen and answer." I knew she was talking about Jesus Christ.

"He'd want to talk with me? Wouldn't he rather just snuff out my existence?" I snapped. Helyn smiled.

"Jesus often ate with sinners, tax-collectors, and thieves. Why not you?"

"So…how do I talk to Him, and how does He answer me?" I queried. I wondered if I was amusing her or asking because I wanted to know. Helyn leaned forward again.

"Prayer is the word we use when we speak about talking to Christ. It's just a fancy word. All I mean is that you should talk to Him like you do me."

"Can I hear him respond?" I asked.

"Yes, but not in the way you think. Christ will answer you by His own means, and in His own time, He won't speak to you as I do."

"So basically, I'm carrying a one-sided conversation," I summed up scornfully.

"No, He's listening and answering. When He does answer, you'll know," Helyn said, encouragingly.

"I'll know how?" I pressed. Helyn's would-be answer was cut off by a sudden commotion in The Enclave. Helyn stood and watched silently as the tents fell, men and women ran from one place to another, and even children scurried about with well-known tasks.

"What's the commotion?" I inquired.

"We're moving," Helyn said. She grabbed her weapon and ran off for some destination. I followed her to the place where a tent might have stood. Naric and another leader were folding it down.

"Get him out of here now. The tyrrohns are advancing, they broke the west unit," Naric commanded. Helyn nodded and ran past me, grabbing my arm. I ran behind her.

"What's going on?"

"The tyrrohns are breaking our defenses and coming for The Enclave. You have to get out of here.

A horse will be faster than running. Do you know how to ride?" Helyn shouted back at me as she vaulted into the horses' holding pen.

"Sure, maybe a few years ago," I replied honestly, slipping in with her.

"It'll have to do. Get up." She flipped a halter and reins on a horse and then looked at me expectantly. I hesitated, then swung myself up onto the horse's back. There was no saddle, but I clutched the reins with white knuckles and instinctively held on with my knees.

"Most of the men are staying to pack up and move, also fight if needed. Women and children are leaving. Just don't ride too crazily. Head south," Helyn instructed, then she turned to leave.

"Wait! What about you? What's the protocol here?" I called. Helyn waved over another girl about her age. The girl hopped on behind me, and I instantly knew I was responsible for getting more than myself away from the tyrrohns.

"Head south, Adrian!" Helyn called back, then she disappeared into the crowd.

"Go," the girl behind me shouted. I kicked the horse, and we took off into the woods. The only way to get around in Chahcan was either by walking or by horse. I used to know how to ride but had fallen out of practice when I took up my wanderings. Nevertheless, I thought I could remember enough to get by. It didn't take me long to get the horse from a walk to a trot and then to a steady canter.

We were at the rear of a large group of Defenders, all women and children, who had taken the other horses. The Defenders who had been required to walk had gone another way. It must have been a strategy put in place years ago. I figured that, so long as I followed the others, we were good. However, even the children pressed their horses so fast I began to fall behind. Then, out of the blue, the Defenders ahead split up, all going in different directions up ahead and disappearing into the forestry. I kept us straight for no good reason.

"Do you know where you're going?" the girl riding with me asked.

"No, I'm trying to figure out where I am." We were having to yell to be heard over the noise of pounding hooves and wind slapping our faces.

"So, now wouldn't be a good time to tell you that we're being followed?" the girl wondered. I glanced back at the pursuing tyrrohns. They, too, had horses.

"Yeah, not really," I agreed.

"Look out! Turn left, turn left!" My head swiveled back just in time to feel the horse pull left on its own accord. We had barely missed running straight into a tree.

"You're Adrian Falkner, right?" the girl asked.

"Yeah, and you?" I inquired distractedly, trying to focus on the path ahead.

"Carissa Harris, a spy for the Defense," she answered.

"Okay. Do you have any idea where South is?"

"No, but I do know that there's an Underground tunnel up ahead, to your left," Carissa said. "So, I suggest turning around." I frowned, trying to concentrate.

"We're going into the Underground," I announced.

"What?" Carissa asked, freaking out.

"The position of the Underground entrance is…"

"We're heading North," Carissa said, answering my question.

"I know the tunnels in there. I know how to get to the south from inside." This statement was more of a half-truth. Or maybe a flat-out lie. I didn't have time to decide at that moment.

"But we won't be able to get out! That's supposed to be an exit, not an entrance!" Carissa blurted out.

"I know," I told her. Carissa stopped arguing as I urged the horse into the tunnel 'entrance.' The Underground was darker than I remembered. We cantered through tunnel after tunnel, taking each turn without hesitation.

"Mind telling me what your plan is?" Carissa asked after a while. I shook my head. I wasn't positive it was there, but I thought I remembered seeing another 'entrance' while being down here before. Of course, I hadn't taken the time to explore it. A noise rose from out of nowhere, a whisper that seemed to surround me.

"What is that?" Carissa demanded.

I knew the sound; it was Death's voice. I shook my head, trying not to listen, but the whispering voice took on words.

"You're running right to me. How foolish. You should have known better than to come into my dominion thinking you could escape," Death taunted. I gripped the reins tighter and took the next turn. Suddenly, Death's figure was in the tunnel, and we were on a straight course to run into him. Carissa screamed. The horse shook its head and hesitated. I gave the horse another kick in the barrel, forcing it to keep going. Just before we ran into him, Death disappeared, and we were free to continue on our way.

"You're going to have to do better than that," I muttered.

"What was that?" Carissa asked.

"It was Death, the enemy. He's trying to get us to stop."

"Then, why are we down here?" It was a good question. It took me a minute to answer.

"Because," I finally said.

"I don't think strategy is your thing," Carissa said. Turning right, I hoped to see what I was looking for. Unfortunately, I was, once again, lost in the tunnels. We kept going, turning into one tunnel after another. Several times the horse dropped from its canter to a walk, and I had to force it to run again. The whisper grew louder again, although it did not take on words.

Abruptly, Death appeared in our path again. This time, the horse spooked, stopping dead in its tracks and rearing a little. Carissa's grip around my stomach tightened and she gasped.

"Dear Lord Jesus Christ..." she murmured in my ear. Instantly, Death's confident figure shuddered and faded away again. The horse calmed down and I cautiously urged it forward. Eventually, we broke into a canter again.

"Adrian, look! Turn left," Carissa burst forth, pointing with a long, slender finger. I did as she told me and found another tunnel entrance, or in this case, exit. Once out of the Underground, the whisper stopped, and we found ourselves in open land. Carissa laughed nervously.

"Huh, who knew? Quick, see that building on our right? Head there, it's another base for the Defense." I turned the horse in that direction and gave it one last kick. As soon as we were close, a gate opened, and we flew inside. I pulled on the reins, and the horse gladly came to a cattle-pony stop. The gate closed behind us, and I slid off the horse. Carissa did the same as I glanced around at the high stone walls that protected us. I looked over at Carissa, who gave me a wide-eyed stare. We both breathed out sighs of relief and then laughed.

"I can't believe that worked," she said.

"I had my doubts," I admitted.

"Being a trained spy, that's not the way I would have done it, but," she hesitated, gave a small laugh, and then shrugged. "Well, you got the job done," Carissa finally said. Once again, I looked around me, taking in new features of the extraordinary fort.

"How come you guys weren't here to begin with?" I asked. "Why would you choose to live in the woods when this offers so much more protection?"

"We're too easy to spot when we are here. During attacks, we come here for protection. Then, we leave again. We try to keep both our enemy and the Ruling Heads guessing where we are. This place is usually abandoned, so no one takes much notice of it."

"I guess that makes sense," I said slowly. As Carissa showed me more of the place, I took the time to look at her more carefully. Her blonde hair was streaked with brown and black, and her green eyes sparkled with life. Her air reminded me of a spy; secretive and stealthy, always on guard. As we toured the whole place, though, I could tell something was bothering her. Finally, she voiced it.

"I don't get it. We're missing all the leaders," Carissa said, with a disappointed tone.

"What about Helyn? She stayed behind," I observed.

"You can't lose me that easily," came a teasing voice behind me. I turned and found Helyn standing there. I grinned at Helyn, glad that she was safe. Carissa ran to her side, and they hugged.

"So, you met Carissa," Helyn observed.

"Okay, I think I'm catching on to how you like to roll. You planned this all along, didn't you?" I asked.

"Planned what? So, tell me. How did you get here safely?"

"I'm not that bad of a rider," I protested. Carissa and I told her our story.

"Not your usual entrance style," Helyn told Carissa, "but not a completely bad idea. Don't worry, the leaders are all accounted for and plan to come after night has fallen."

"Praise the Lord! Did we lose anyone?" Carissa wanted to know. Helyn shrugged, palms up.

"Not that I know of. Howard's kinship is reported with Titus' just outside Veaus. Our riders distracted them from our second and third groups."

"And the men got all the supplies housed?" Carissa continued to pry. Helyn nodded.

"They weren't required to fight, so there was plenty of time to get the things hidden. I think Adrian's flight distracted them."

"Oh, good," Carissa quipped.

"That had better be sarcastic," I shot back. Carissa raised her eyebrows but said nothing. "And did you say, 'kinship,' Helyn?"

"Yes," Helyn answered brightly. "Each of the seven leaders is primarily responsible for a certain number of Defenders, a kinship. Under the leaders are the commanders of our armies, who are all under Naric's direct leadership."

"I think you confused him," Carissa noted. Helyn laughed.

"I see that. Sorry," she apologized.

"Since you have all the answers, why don't you tell me where Alex ended up?" I challenged.

"You've got me there. My best guess would be somewhere in the Fort," Helyn replied.

"Okay, one last question: what happens now?" I queried.

"I'll answer that one," Carissa piped up. "The Defense will be staying here for a few days, so you train, of course."

# CHAPTER SEVEN

## Buried in the Ground

Alex had come on another horse, but his ride had been much less eventful. When the leaders came sometime after midnight, the Defencio Veritas decided to settle for the night. Because of the enormous width of the Fort's walls, thousands of rooms had been erected inside them. Alex and I shared a room with a family who had two boys just younger than us. I wasn't sure whose idea that was, but Helyn was a prime suspect in my book. When morning dawned, the women hurried to prepare a large meal in the multiple kitchens which the Fort had. Meanwhile, the leaders convened in one of the eight towers. At last, the leaders came down and announced we were staying. They didn't say for how long.

With everyone safe inside the Fort, Robert began training with Alex and me once again. The training happened in the middle of the Fort. It was a roped off area, about a third of the size of the Center of The Enclave. This time, Robert handed Alex and me wooden swords with the instructions to fight each other. Alex looked at the sword in surprise and then to Helyn, who was sitting a few feet away watching.

"Come on," I encouraged. Alex took up the challenge. He swung the sword at me wildly, and I blocked it with ease. Again and again, he swung at me. I blocked each hit and then launched out at him. In five strokes, I had 'killed' him.

I looked at Robert. "Want to join the fight?" I asked him. Robert shook his head.

"Go again. You're doing good," he said. I turned back slowly to Alex.

"Come on. Be faster and more aggressive or…do you want to look bad in front of Helyn?" I taunted. Alex was instantly inspired and tried to mimic my technique. I blocked one of his hits and then spun around, kicking him down and pointing my wooden blade at his throat.

"You're making me look bad," Alex protested.

"Isn't that the point?"

"Well done, Adrian. Colin must have taught you a thing or two," Robert said, chuckling. "Go again." Alex and I fought for the next half hour, and I won every time. Helyn stopped watching after the fifth round. After another hour of one-on-one training with Robert, Alex went off to find Helyn, and Robert went to help another student. For two days, I saw Robert for sword training, that is, unless he was called away by other amateur students who accidentally shot an arrow into one of the horses' stalls.

+++++++

"Okay, today is the day," Colin announced. After three days in the Fort, the Defense had moved back into the woods, somewhere between Copper Ridge and Vainus. The kinships which had hidden in Veaus rejoined our larger group. The tents were all back up, I was again staying at Nahum's, and the Center had been reconstructed, this time on the eastern side of The Enclave.

"Today is the day for what?" I asked Colin. After spending the last several days with Robert, Naric had decided that I should give him a break and let Colin take me on. Alex chose to let someone else teach him to better handle his axe, rather than leap around.

"I finally get to shoot some arrows at you and see if you can dodge them," Colin said, excitedly. I gave him a wide-eyed stare.

"Uh, is that safe?"

"Where's the fun in safe?" he asked, then laughed. "Yes, perfectly safe. Remember, I'm going to put the ball on the end."

"Oh, right," I said. "The idea sounds cool in theory, but with that weight on it, won't the arrow just fall to the ground?" Colin picked up a bow and two arrows, then produced a ball.

"On the contrary, this ball won't affect the flight of the arrow at all." Colin gave me a sideways glance and a grin. "For the withstanding reason that I took the middle out of the ball, and it weighs little to nothing now."

"Oh. Why don't you just take the tip off the arrow?"
I questioned.

Colin laughed. "I'm pretty sure disassembling
weapons is against some sort of rule," he mentioned.
"It wouldn't do for all our archers to line up in battle
only to find the tips gone from their arrows." He did a
mock scene, pretending to try and shoot, then realizing
there was no tip. His eyes widened dramatically. I
laughed.

"Okay," I agreed.

"Get ready," Colin ordered. He lined up and stuck
the ball on the tip. I stood about five yards away from
him. I had about ten feet of space before I might run
into the other fifty-seven students training in agility.
The hum of voices, grunts, and praise blended into an
indistinct tone which I could easily ignore.

"I'm going to fire it straight at you," Colin warned.
I readied myself to jump out of the way. Colin drew
back the string with the arrow. The minute he let go,
I jumped to my left and dropped to the ground. The
arrow sailed harmlessly into the brush behind me. I
stared at the thing, breathing hard.

"You good?" Colin asked as I got up.

"Something about you shooting at me just doesn't
seem right," I said, then grinned at him. "Do it again."
Colin laughed.

"Alright," he consented.

The longer Colin shot at me, the better I got,
and the more fun it was. He taught me several new

techniques for getting out of the way. I even went so far as to let him shoot at me while my back was turned. Eventually, Colin called it a day.

"I don't know about you," Colin told me, "but that was fun. I should shoot arrows at my students more often." Then, he chuckled nervously. "I guess that would be too much fun, eh?" I laughed along with him.

Grabbing my sword on the way, I walked out of the Center and almost ran into Nahum.

"Ready for some Faze Whip training? Brought your Whip." He tossed me the weapon. I grabbed it in exchange for my sword, and we headed off into the woods.

"So, what do your parents do?" Nahum asked as I worked on using the Faze Whip.

"Dad's a merchant. I can't remember what Mom does," I answered briefly. We were 'battling' each other. Nahum struck out, and I dodged. It was my turn to move first. I got close and used the weapon like you would a double-sided sword.

"How long have you been in the Defense, Nahum?"

"Four years," Nahum said, shoving me away from him. I unlocked the Whip, swung it out, he dodged, and the Whip snapped back together. Nahum nodded his approval as I locked the Whip again. Then, he jumped toward me and struck with his Whip. I deflected the blow and backed away.

"What did your parents do?" I asked.

"They were both teachers. Father served time as a spy," Nahum said, striking for my feet. I jumped and swung at him at the same time, missing by a few inches. Nahum spun his Faze Whip in quick circles and forced me backward. I unlocked the weapon and tried to strike at him, but he avoided by unlocking his Whip and jumping up into a tree above my head.

"What are your parents like?" he wondered. Nahum used the Whip to drop silently from the tree, and we stood at a standoff.

"Mom's good. She cooks a lot and tries to be a peacemaker. Dad hates me. He's always angry at me," I said, readying myself for an attack.

"No," Nahum said calmly. Then, he ran forward and pushed me back with force. Swinging in a series of moves, he tripped me and I sprawled on my back. Nahum pressed one of the Damascus blades to my chest.

"Don't fool yourself. He loves you." His serene tone didn't resemble the fire in his brown eyes. Nahum pulled his weapon away and walked into the woods. A minute later, he disappeared.

"What got into him?"

+++++++

Later in the day, I met up with Alex, who had plenty of things to tell me about how to properly wield an axe.

We ate lunch together, taking our food to the Center to sit.

"You sure your parents are okay with you being here?" Alex wondered.

"Why do you care?" I growled. Alex bit into his meat and shrugged.

"Well, I know my parents are fine with it, but they think I'm at your place. I don't want Bridge telling on us," he commented.

"Your parents won't take Bridge's word," I argued.

"Yours might," Alex said around a mouthful of food. I shook my head and took a drink.

"Dad's on a business trip, and Mom's too busy to notice," I retorted.

"Alright, that's good enough for me," Alex said. We had been in The Enclave for about eighteen days straight. Even Helyn had gone back to her parents' house for many of those days. However, she had caring, involved parents, unlike Alex and me. Alex set down his cup and gestured in front of him.

"Hey, look. Here comes Helyn," he announced. Sure enough, she was coming across the Center toward us, dodging the hundreds of drilling Defenders.

"When you guys are finished," Helyn began, before she even reached us, "Naric and Robert are waiting in the Tent of Meetings. We're supposed to meet them there."

"Where's the Tent of Meetings?" I asked, swallowing my last bite.

Helyn chuckled. "You've been there before," she hinted.

"Then, I guess I'm lost," Alex asserted.

"It's the largest tent in the camp where the Leaders usually convene. It's about half a mile from here, so we'd better get walking," Helyn explained. Alex and I nodded.

"We're done. You can lead the way," Alex said.

"Sure. Oh, by the way, Nahum's meeting us there, too." Helyn looked over her shoulder and smiled knowingly. Helyn led the way without faltering or asking questions.

"How do you always know where you're going?" I asked her. The Enclave had been erected in three different places and three separate ways in just over two weeks. I still needed help finding Nahum's tent occasionally.

"Well, there's a rule concerning the whereabouts of the Tent of Meetings. It must be within two miles of every kinship in The Enclave. So, each set up leaves the Tent of Meetings in about the center."

"Unlike the inaccurately named Center," Alex quipped.

"Inaccurate?" Helyn posed cheerily. "It is there that we train our men for battle and our women to defend themselves. We build each other with the Holy Scriptures, growing in our belief every day. And we teach the next generation all these things. Our lives are centered around the instruction that comes there."

"She's got you there," I said. Alex sulked. His attempts to impress Helyn were failing terribly. After a few minutes of silent walking, we entered the Tent of Meetings and found Nahum, just as promised, along with Naric and Robert. Again, a man was standing in the corner with a blank stare, as if he didn't care what was going on around him.

"Ah, good. You're all here," Robert said eagerly. "The last time we sent you three down to the Underground, Death revealed himself. Commander Naric and I have decided it would be good to send you four down there."

"For what purpose?" Nahum asked.

"To draw Death out and track his movements."

"So, this isn't a battle, this is a scouting mission," Nahum clarified. Robert nodded.

"Just remember that Death must appear," Naric added.

*Great, I feel like bait,* I inwardly moaned.

"Stick together, keep each other safe, and don't let the enemy suspect your purpose," Robert instructed. We all nodded.

"Let's go," Nahum said, taking the lead to the portal. Helyn, Alex, and I grabbed our weapons on the way out, and Nahum gathered a lantern for each of us to carry. Going back to the Underground wasn't a welcome mission. I regretted the decision as soon as the portal closed overhead, leaving us in the black tunnels. The four of us lit our lanterns moved in, wandering through the confusing tunnels. Nahum let me take the lead.

"So, are we supposed to just wait him out?" I asked, aware of how unsure I sounded. Helyn shrugged.

"I guess," she replied. "Then, do we fight Death? I mean…" I turned around and motioned for her to be silent. Helyn obeyed, flashing me a confused look. Then, she heard it too, and her eyes widened. We all extinguished our lanterns and pulled out our weapons. The sound grew closer and louder. It was a whisper, but it was enough to send chills up my spine. I knew who the voice belonged to. For the longest time, nothing showed, and waiting for the haunting figure to show built the tension inside me. Suddenly, he was standing right in front of us, his ice-blue eyes staring me down. We all jumped and aimed our weapons at him. He didn't seem the least bit concerned.

"Have you come back to fight me?" Death aimed his words at me. "Surely not, when I offer you freedom. The freedom to be who you want to be."

"I'm already who I want to be," I answered.

"Yes, you were always meant to be with the Defense. It was always meant to get you here," Death agreed.

"Now, there's something unexpected. What do you mean by that?" I asked.

"You were always meant for something else." His voice made my skin crawl. He seemed to know something I didn't. I raised my weapon, ready to strike.

"Just come out and say what you mean," I challenged.

"Weren't you always meant to save your sister?" came the reply. I stopped in my intended attack, unable to move myself or my blade. My heart pounded in my ears as I watched Death step to the side, and two dark figures brought forward a girl with her hands bound. My eyes glued to the prisoner. She lifted her head, and I couldn't breathe. Those beautiful, innocent blue eyes, the golden hair, and the flawless skin could only belong to one person.

"Miriam," I whispered breathlessly. She saw me and flashed a smile my way, full and perfect.

"Adrian, help me," she called, her tone implying that she was fully trusting in my ability to save her. I wanted to jump forward and bring my sword down on top of those men. Then, I wanted to grasp her hand again and take her away. Instead, I stared helplessly at Miriam's face, unable to move.

"Go on, save her," Death prodded. He was so close I could feel his breath on my neck.

"Adrian Falkner, a little help?" Helyn called, her voice strained. Sounds of clanging metal, others shouting, and deep grunts surrounded me. I knew something was going on behind me. I was even semi-conscious that I ought to turn around and help Helyn, but I couldn't take my gaze off Miriam.

"Snap out of it!" Alex's voice was distant.

"Just try to save your sister. She won't be taken easily," Death taunted me.

*What's wrong with me? Why won't I move?*

Miriam's blue eyes looked into mine pleadingly, yet she was shaking her head.

"Adrian!" I heard Nahum's voice just before I got slammed onto the ground. I felt as if I had just woken up. Above me, one of Death's men screamed as he brought his weapon down toward me.

"Whoa!" I shouted, rolling quickly out of the way. Helyn ran toward me, grabbing my arm and then pulling me on.

"Come on, we have to get out of here," she called. I jerked my arm from her grasp.

"Wait!" I protested. Nahum shoved me forward.

"Now is not the time, Adrian," he said. I looked back at the place, which swarmed with dark figures now, and got one last look at Miriam. Those bright blue eyes watched me leave.

+++++++

I was silent while Nahum, Alex, and Helyn explained Death's appearance and the fight. Naric watched and listened, and, when they finished their explanation, his piercing eyes found me.

"And where was Adrian in all this?" he asked.

"In his own world," Alex answered. Naric ignored his answer; he wanted mine. I sighed and tried to explain.

"I...he had...I couldn't move, I don't know it's just like...he..." I stammered.

"Think harder," came Naric's unrelenting tone. It became clear to me that he was challenging my reliability. He was wondering whose side I was truly on. I glared at him.

"Death has my sister, okay?" I fired at him.

"Your sister?" Alex asked confusedly. "I thought you were an only child."

"I was never an only child," I muttered, thinking aloud.

"What happened to your sister?" Helyn wondered. I struggled to hold back my welling emotions and shook my head. What happened? Did I even know what had honestly happened?

"I don't know," I huffed. Naric seemed to be on the verge of saying something, but changed his mind and left. The other three stood around me as if waiting for a better answer.

"I don't want to talk about this," I said, whirling around and running away. Miriam's perfect, bright personality filled my mind. How did Death have her? It didn't make sense.

After Morro had left us, Miriam had held our family together. Unknowingly, of course. She had only been four at the time. She was our light, our joy, our hope—the one person we all could love without holding back. Miriam had only lived seven years before an incurable illness had taken over her body.

After Mom and Dad had figured out there was no cure, Miriam was sent away. I only saw her once more before she died in my arms.

I leaned against a tree and sobbed.

"Why? I don't understand. Why did you send her away?" I thought aloud as if screaming to my parents. "It wasn't fair!" I sobbed until I couldn't anymore and then sank to the ground, putting my head between my knees.

Miriam's death had been the final breaking point in my family. Three years hadn't been enough time to heal the sorrow and pain of losing Miriam. I figured there was nothing that could cure it. After all, I would never be able to forget walking into Bridge's Mansion for the first time after Miriam had died and hearing Bridge's lecture about 'God's punishment for sin is death.' The haunting thought I had fought off for the last two years came back.

*It's your fault, Adrian. You know what sin is, and stealing is definitely on that list. Your sin caused Miriam to die!*

"No," I gasped out, shaking my head. "I loved her. I can't live with the thought of killing her!"

Night fell, and I walked to the Center. It was empty. I welcomed the loneliness and camped out in the deserted place for the night.

# CHAPTER EIGHT

## When the Heart Bleeds

"Adrian, what are you doing here?" Nahum's voice made me shake from my drowsy, thinking state. I glanced behind me. The Center was swarming with Defenders, all working on completing their various tasks. As I turned my gaze back into the endless forestry beyond The Enclave, Nahum sat beside me, his Faze Whip still in his hand. I hadn't ever seen him without it.

"You didn't come back yesterday. You seem very disturbed and discouraged," Nahum mentioned. I nodded, rubbing my eyes wearily. "Want to talk about it?"

"What's there to talk about?" I growled.

"How about your sister?" Nahum suggested. I glared at the ground beneath my feet.

For some reason, the words just fell from my lips.

"Miriam died at seven years of age from a contagious and incurable disease. She was a light and she was perfect. Somehow, she's now Death's prisoner," I blurted out.

"There's something more. Right?" Nahum pressed. My head snapped up, and I wondered how he could read me.

"My past is nothing but hurt, and it's nothing I'm proud of. I don't want to be reliving it. When I came to fight, I didn't think that all this would unfold," I spat out angrily.

"You were told, I'm sure, that you would change," Nahum replied calmly.

"Yeah, Helyn told me, but I didn't think that meant I would have to face everything in my life all over again!"

"Your past circumstances shape you, Adrian. If you're going to change, you have to deal with your past. That's just the way it works. I should know." Something in his voice quelled my anger against him. Nahum rose and brandished his weapon. "I'll see you tomorrow? For Faze Whip training, right?"

"Sure," I agreed. Nahum flashed a rare smile and departed. I thought I was alone again, but Helyn's voice proved me wrong.

"I wish I knew how to help," she said. I whirled around to face the girl. Her gentle compassion was a surprise to me.

"Why?" I questioned her, crossly. Helyn honestly looked hurt by my tone this time.

"Because I know the One who will bring comfort. It is what friends do for each other. They are waiting to know the way to help and then act on it," she explained.

"How can you keep saying things like that?" I wondered, my tone a touch softer. "I'm a liar, a thief, and a trespasser, and you still talk like...that."

Although my confession was new to Helyn, she didn't miss a beat.

"Because I believe that any man can change," Helyn said. "God will take a thief and make him a giver. He'll take a liar and make him speak life. He'll take a trespasser and make his feet walk upon holy ground." Her words stung. I stood and sighed.

"I'll be late meeting up with Colin," I mentioned, hurrying away from her.

+++++++

Alex and I walked into the Center the next day and, after a quick look around, found that neither Robert nor Colin were there.

"So, now we wait for Helyn to come along," Alex said, sitting on the ground.

"Oh, yeah, right." I rolled my eyes. "You know it's a hopeless cause."

"Never say never," Alex replied. After a few minutes, I spotted Robert and Colin walking together. They were so deep in conversation that they passed Alex and me with only one glance. I stared after them for a moment and then leapt to my feet to follow them.

"Where are you going?" Alex moaned. Then, he sighed and followed me. Robert's glance was enough for me to want to know, at the least, if they were talking about me. My two instructors took a course that skirted the perimeter of The Enclave. Alex and I followed them close enough to hear, but out of sight behind trees and tents. However, it seemed impossible to skirt the other Defenders. Despite our obvious attempt to spy on the two leaders, no one stopped us. Eventually, I got close enough to catch full sentences.

"She told you, too?" Robert sounded surprised.

"I'm a good confident," Colin replied.

"Well, of course, I know that. So, what do you think?"

"We all knew he'd have issues."

"Sure. Do you still think it'll work out?" Robert posed. There was a short pause.

"What is Adrian's response to the Gospel?" Colin inquired.

"Well, he listens. It's the first step, but I haven't seen much beyond that."

"He's working through a lot, according to Helyn's account. I think she may be right; his quest may take more time," Colin responded. Robert sighed.

"Do you think it's still safe to have him here?"

"What do you mean?"

"Well, we still have to think of what's best for the Defenders as a whole. He could inflict harm."

"Ha! This is coming from a master swordsman," Colin joked.

"Alright, you know what I mean. With Death on this kid's trail, we've got to be careful. Give me your answer honestly," Robert insisted. The two walked on in silence, and I closed the distance to make sure I heard Colin's response.

"I don't know," he finally said. The answer smacked me in the face, and I stopped. The two walked away, but I didn't have the curiosity to hear anything more. Alex had, surprisingly, kept up pretty well and now looked at me with a glance akin to confusion.

"What are you thinking?" he asked. I simply stared at the retreating figures of the leaders. They couldn't trust me. Worse than that, they didn't even know if I was safe to keep around the Defense. Furthermore, Helyn had told them everything. Did she trust me? I shook my head and let out a frustrated yell. I turned and sprinted away, running past the tents and out into the woods beyond.

"Adrian, wait!" Alex called after me, but I didn't stop. I ran without completely knowing where I was or where I would end up. Eventually, my burning legs and lungs stopped me, and I was forced to assess my direction. Miles of untamed forestry which dominated Chahcan's land faced me. My heart pounded and my chest heaved. Where could I go? At last, I decided to find my way back to Copper Ridge.

All day long I hiked through the woods, alternating between running and walking. By the time I reached the old road which led home, I was weak with hunger and thirst. I hurried to my house. There were no lights on, so I slipped in quietly.

Gratefully, I took advantage of the food Mom had in our ice box. I took it into my bedroom and locked my door. Alone once again in a world full of people who didn't know who I was, I resolved to forget.

+ + + + + + +

*Er, er, er, er, er-rck, rck, rck, rck.*
I lay in bed, wide awake, staring at the ceiling. I hardly flinched at the sound of that obnoxious rooster. Something was clearly wrong. Mom had never come home last night. I had dreaded meeting her, yet counted on seeing her. For hours, I'd lain awake trying to decide what to tell her, and, for some reason, I had never given up waiting for her to come. Now, I looked out the window and suddenly remembered what day it was. Thursday. Ledo practice. I pulled myself out of bed, put on clothes that might have been clean, and walked to Bridge's Mansion. I made it through the lectures without knowing what I should have learned or acknowledging anyone that was around me. I slipped in slightly late and slunk out early so Bridge wouldn't have a chance to question me.

Once the lectures ended, I made for the Ledo field. Most of the guys were already on the field. James and I walked together from Bridge's Mansion.

"Where have you been, Adrian?" he asked.

"Uh, I was busy."

"Your pa put you to work?" James wanted to know, as we stepped onto the field. I shook my head. James opened his mouth to ask another question. Then, we both stopped in the middle of the field, staring in front of us.

"Are you seeing what I'm seeing?" James muttered.

"I wish I wasn't," I growled. Standing in front of us was unmistakably Blake Rileder. "Did we need another player?" I inquired of James.

"Unfortunately, yeah," James sighed. Blake turned with a grin.

"Well, well. Adrian Falkner came back. Who would have guessed he would have the nerve?" he taunted. Then, he came closer and hissed under his breath, "I told you, I'd get revenge."

"If you want revenge, why didn't you join the other team and try to take me down?" I challenged. James backed away from us.

"You think I don't know you?" Blake scoffed "Come on, Falkner, you love to lead. Well, I'm leading now. Haven't you heard? I'm superior to you."

"I seriously doubt that," I snapped, remembering how I had hit Colin first try accidentally.

"Doubt all you want, but you can't change the truth," Blake said.

"You're only superior at failing," I retorted, then ran out to my position. Blake lined up to my far left, at the other edge of the field.

*Good. Far enough away that he can't cause me any trouble.*

James lined up beside me, and the other team called over to see if we were ready. We were. In an instant, the game was on. The other team had the ball, and their player rushed toward us. I took off in a sprint, keeping my eyes on the guy with the ball. A person from the other team came up to block me. I spun out of his way and then bowled through the next guy. The ball moved from one person to another on their team until, somehow, Blake managed to get a hold of the ball. It didn't take long for the other team to tackle him to the ground. I was there in an instant.

"Get rid of the ball!" I shouted at him. Blake glared at me defiantly. James rushed up and shouted the same thing. Blake reluctantly gave the ball up to James, who took off at lightning speed. The other team chased him, and most of our team ran to block. I stayed put, and Blake rose to his feet.

"Get off the field, Falkner, this is my team now," Blake growled. I silently stared at him. I wanted to take him on. Wrath and confusion of the past several days burned within me and Blake was there asking for it. So, I tackled him. We fell to the ground, and I landed on top of him. I had enough time to punch him solidly once before he rolled and was then on top of me. I punched him in the face, moved to the right, and, as soon as he was off me, I leapt to my feet.

Blake stood up. He didn't hesitate for a second, running forward and swinging his arm at me. Using the fundamental agility skills I had learned, I dodged each one of his intended hits. Some of the boys had figured out what was going on and gathered around, cheering on the fight. I could see the anger mounting Blake's face each time I moved out of the way. Finally, I took up the offense. I kicked Blake in the stomach, punched him in the face, and then kicked his legs out from under him.

As Blake stood to his feet, I jumped around behind him and kicked him in the back. Blake stumbled forward a few steps, kept his balance, and turned around to swing a punch at me. I moved just in time to miss getting smacked. Then, while his arm was still extended from the blow, I grabbed his arm and jerked him off his feet. I kneed him in the chest and then punched him, sending him flying backward. I took another step toward him, but James suddenly rushed between the two of us.

"Adrian, Adrian! Stop! Do you want to kill him?" he protested. I stood for one-second, breathing hard. Then, I huffed, whirled around, and ran off the field. I sprinted home and, checking to make sure I didn't see anyone there, flew inside. I dashed to my room, locking the door behind me, and sat at the desk, staring blankly at the papers on it.

*I should have hit him a few more times. Maybe I should have killed him. Blake asked for it!*

Thoughts about the fight soon vanished, and new ones arose. I saw Miriam's face and heard the words she had spoken to me. *Is she alive? If so, how do I save her?*

Morro's features came up to haunt me. The record he had left me with had now separated me from the Defense and any chance I had to fight Death or free myself from being called a 'tyrrohn ally.'

*Why can't I just fight Death when he comes? Why do I wait around for him to say something more that will flip my world and goals?*

Eventually, the whirlwind of thoughts calmed down. I stood to my feet, and something on my desk caught my attention—a handwritten note laid on top of the unfinished studies. Curious, I picked it up and read the message.

*'Meet in Walter's Alley to talk.'*

I grimaced at the mention of the place where I had met Morro the night we…no, I had gotten caught. I looked over the note again. No one had signed it.

*Who am I meeting?*

The slant of the handwriting made me instinctively think of the Defense. It was the same hand which the note in the back of Fighters from Ancient Days was written in. Part of me wanted to go and hear what this Defender had to say, and the other part of me didn't want to go anywhere near Walter's Alley.

*It's not like when you went to see Morro,* I told myself. *You won't have to face that conflict. Well, then fine.*

I sighed, grabbed my coat, and headed out for the destination.

# CHAPTER NINE

## Cry for the Lost

Days had grown cool enough to call it autumn, with August gone and September seeping into Copper Ridge. I reached my destination quickly, an alley in the better part of town. Walter's Alley looked more threatening at dusk than it ever had at midnight all those times I had met Morro. Hands in my coat pockets, I searched for the person who had summoned me. The alley had a cobblestoned street and was wide enough for two horses to fit in side by side. Two large, abandoned buildings closed in the space. On one side was an uncommonly used road, on the other, the main road lined with small businesses. The sun was setting behind one of the buildings, leaving the alley dark and shadowy. I shuddered, not wanting to relive another nighttime scene there.

"I hadn't expected you so early," came a voice behind me. I spun around to spot a hooded figure. I knew who the voice belonged to. Frowning, I turned to leave.

"No, wait. Please," Helyn pleaded. She removed the hood, letting her brown hair fall in waves. I paused and turned back.

"I heard you from a mile away, you aren't too hard to track," she said, attempting to tease me.

"This place kind of has a bad history with me," I told her.

"Sorry," she said apologetically. Another hooded figure dropped silently to the ground behind her. I could tell by the weapon that it was Nahum. Helyn took a minute to look me over. "So, how was Ledo practice?" she queried, with an amused smile. I suddenly remembered that I hadn't cleaned up.

"Oh, uh, fine," I answered. Helyn nodded.

"I'll bet your parents are glad to see you're safe and all that," she said.

"They don't know I'm here," I replied sharply. Helyn suddenly lost her smile.

"Then, why did you leave?" For a long moment, that question hung in the air. Helyn continued, "The leaders have become confused. The Defenders keep wondering what happened. You just disappeared without so much as an explanation. Naric feared we might not find you again." Once more, she waited for me to speak. I refused to look at her.

"Adrian," Helyn sighed. "We know that the revealing of your past was the last thing you wanted, but you've been called. You accepted, and you've been doing well. We didn't even know who Death was until you came along. You've given us the hope I believe you were intended to bring. You have to help us finish the fight."

"Why do I have to help you finish the fight? Why am I so important to you? And don't tell me that it's because of the calling," I added.

"You're worth more to the Defense than you know," Helyn replied. I glanced at Nahum, remembering his words to me in our first meeting. "Do you remember," Helyn continued, "when we first spoke to you of the quest? When I said you would face things that would turn you from your goal?"

"I can't even see my goal anymore," I argued.

"Adrian Falkner, there is still hope among Defenders that you are the one called by God to defeat Death," Helyn steadily responded.

"I can't! I can't even fight him anymore. You've seen me when he comes. I freeze, and he always has time to show me something I don't want to see," I shot back.

Nahum spoke up for the first time, "You can be taught to resist the enemy and his words. You will defeat Death."

"No, he's too great a challenge," I fought.

"He is not. Adrian, I know you have what is needed. A fire within, talent, and strength. You're the hero," Nahum pointed out. I shook my head.

"I'm a thief," I said quietly. Nahum and Helyn were silent for a minute. Helyn stared past me until she spoke again.

"We are friends, aren't we?" she asked. I didn't need to consider this.

"Yes."

"Then, hear my words: you can't just give up. You're a fighter. Death is still targeting you, what will be your answer?"

"Death has my sister," I objected. Helyn sighed.

"I don't know about that, Adrian," she said sadly. "While she might appear to be alive, I'm sure she will leave when Death is defeated." The thought that Miriam might be lost to me again made my stomach drop.

"If he is what keeps her alive, by some strange power, then I can't kill him. I can't see Miriam die again."

"We don't know that she's actually alive," Nahum mentioned. "What if he's just playing with you?"

"What if he's not?" I posed. Helyn wrapped her arms around her body.

"Sister or no sister, this quest is yours. We'll stand by you until you have finished it, but we won't let you give up!" she passionately cried. I tried to avoid her gaze and found Nahum's brown eyes searching my face.

"Why did you accept the quest, Adrian?" he asked. The question smacked me in the face, and I took a step back. For a moment, I figured I would just say what they wanted to hear. Then, I decided I was tired of lying to them.

"To get even with the tyrrohns and...to clear my name. I didn't want to be a tyrrohn ally," I answered.

"Now?" Nahum pressed.

"I can't give up on Miriam! Don't you get it? She died once because of me, and I'm not going to let her die again!"

"Because of you?" Helyn gasped. Nahum stepped closer.

"So, this is it? You have no intention to follow through," he accused. I glared at him.

"You two go kill Death. I mean, you have everything figured out already. Save the Defense and be the heroes." Helyn and Nahum exchanged glances. When Helyn looked at me again, her eyes were filled with tears.

"I still don't want you to give up, but…but you're too determined to think of yourself," she snapped. Helyn whirled around, pulled the hood over her head, and walked away. Nahum tapped a Damascus blade of his Faze Whip on the ground twice.

"I thought I'd found a friend," he said. Then, Nahum was also gone. With one last glance around the old, haunting alley, I left.

I swiftly made my way back to my house, running down the old dirt road as I fumed against myself and the Defense. I pounded up the steps and entered the house, racing for my bedroom.

"Stop." Mom's voice turned me around. Her blonde hair was pulled back tightly, and her blue eyes were trained solely on me. "Adrian Falkner, where have you been?"

"Taking a vacation of sorts," I mumbled, immediately knowing it was a lame excuse. Mom was clearly unimpressed.

"Vacation?" she scoffed. "Really, Adrian, what in the Fallen Lands have you been doing?" I didn't answer. Seeing Mom home had brought a sudden relief, but also the old feeling of defiance. Mom sighed. "I was so worried that you wouldn't come back. Please, Adrian, I need to know what you've been doing. Because you haven't been here and I know you haven't been at Alex's place; Alex hasn't been at his place either. Where are you staying?" Mom pressed.

"At the base of the secret fighters in the woods several miles away," I replied, my voice low. The mention of the place and the fighters made me feel guilty. I remembered Helyn's wounded look and Nahum's disappointed tone.

"Adrian, stop talking nonsense. I want an answer," Mom said.

"I'm not talking nonsense," I persisted. Mom sighed and stuck a piece of chocolate in her mouth. She savored the bite for a minute. It seemed ironic that I was aggravated with Mom for thinking that I would be doing just what I had been doing to her for the past three years; lying.

"I want nothing but the truth," Mom said calmly. "All I need to know is where you have been staying and what you have been doing."

*You wouldn't believe me if I told you I've been facing Death,* I thought. Then, added aloud, "I've already told you: I've been with a group of secret fighters that have a base in the woods of Chahcan."

"You're not going to convince me any more than the tyrrohns can, Adrian Falkner. I will not be distracted from getting what I want." Mom raised her voice.

"But they are real. The tyrrohns really are looking for them, hoping to draw them from their hiding place so they can defeat them. They stay in hiding because the Ruling Heads don't want them to fight," I elaborated, hoping she might believe me.

"Adrian Falkner!" Mom exclaimed. "You're already in trouble with Bridge for your absence, and your father claims you're in trouble with him. You cannot be in trouble with the Ruling Heads, too."

"I'm already in trouble with the Ruling Heads. Tyrrohn ally, remember?" I shot back. Mom's eyebrows raised. "Just like Morro," I added.

"Not quite like Morro," Mom argued. "Unlike Morro, you cannot be a wanted man!" I glared at her for a few seconds and then ran to my room, slamming my door and locking it behind me.

# CHAPTER TEN

## Burden of the Fallen

Two days after my fight with Mom, I slipped from the house and back into the woods of Chahcan. It was now clear what I had to do. I may have been willing to let Death live on with his dark warriors, but there was no way I'd let him have Miriam, too. It was time to take my sister back. I had no doubt that Death wouldn't let her go without a fight, so I planned to sneak into The Enclave, grab my sword, and then make for the Underground. I surprised myself by noticing marks in the trees and winding my way to The Enclave without falter. Crouching in the brush, I waited until night descended, and most of the Defenders had retired. Once the moon shed its silver light upon the clearings, I leapt from my hiding spot. The Center was relatively still; only two men chatted at the bow rack. I dashed for the swords and grabbed one, fastening the scabbard around my waist. A glance at the two men assured me that I was unnoticed. Keeping my eyes on them, I took off running again. *Smack!* My head collided with a tree and I fell flat on my back.

"Ow," I groaned under my breath.

"I didn't think you'd come back." The voice made me jump to my feet and glance wildly around.

"Nahum," I hissed. "Why do you have to sneak up on me like that?"

"Because it's fun," he smirked. "Especially with you." I glowered and chose to ignore his last sentence. Nahum spun his FazeWhip around in a smooth circle. His brown eyes searched my face. "So, what are you doing?"

"I, uh, figured it was time Death got a good beating," I decided to say. Nahum's eyebrows raised.

"You're going alone?" he queried.

"Well, I didn't think you all wanted to come with me...after...you know," I stammered. Nahum stilled his weapon.

"Adrian, we're with you. I'll gather a team, and we'll meet you at the nearest portal. You remember how to get there?" he asked. I nodded. Nahum turned to go, then glanced over his shoulder and added, "I was hoping you wouldn't give up." Nahum left, and I hurried to the portal. I wasn't going to wait around for the team to show up. I cleared fresh leaves and twigs from the metal plate and lifted the hatch. Adjusting the sword, I swung onto the ladder, and rushed down, closing the portal behind me. Just as I reached the bottom, the hatch lifted, and others scurried down the ladder. I sighed and waited. Helyn came down first, cloaked in a dark cape, and carrying her bow. Alex was next, wielding his axe and scowling like an angry bear.

"Well, if I were Death, I wouldn't mess with you," I quipped, looking at Alex.

"And don't you doubt it," Alex muttered.

"Let's go," Helyn spoke up.

"Nahum?" I asked, cocking my head to look up at the portal, which was closed again. Helyn shook her head.

"Never you mind," she said. I nodded and confidently entered the tunnels. Team or no team, my mission was the same. We were entirely silent as we walked through the tunnels. I knew where I wanted to go, and the others followed. Finally, we stepped into a large room, carved in a circular shape. Despite what I was expecting, the room was empty. I frowned and walked around the room, keeping close to the walls. Helyn and Alex were looking at me weird.

"What are you doing?" Helyn whispered. I walked another circle peering carefully at every detail in the dirt walls.

"Looking for something like...this." I knelt and studied the small door I had just found. "It's big enough to go through, come on," I said, opening the door and beginning to go through.

"What? And trap ourselves so that Death can find us easier?" Alex asked. I ignored him and scanned the darkness I had crawled into. I heard the others crawling in behind me. At the back of the room, chained to the wall, was the figure of my sister.

"Miriam," I whispered as I came closer. Her bright head lifted, and her blue eyes found me.

"Adrian." I barely recognized the tone of her voice. I went over to the chains and attempted to get them off.

"Hang on, Miriam. I'm getting you out of here," I whispered.

"You can't," she said, her voice flat. As dread settled in my gut, I longingly searched her blue eyes.

"What are you talking about?"

"I'm an illusion. Death is using my supposed presence to draw you here. I thought you might have guessed that." Miriam's tone was sweet and childish, but the words stung. I clenched my hands tightly around the chains.

"How is that even possible?" Alex inquired. "I mean, we can see you."

"Yes, you should," Miriam nodded. "Listen. Death takes men's souls and then they must serve him. Those are the ones you call 'tyrrohns.' They are eternally bound in hell, though they appear alive to you, as well."

"How come you aren't like one of those shadows?" Alex queried.

"Because Death does not own my soul," Miriam answered. She looked at me, her features softening. "Don't you know where my soul is?" I shook my head.

"Is your soul in heaven?" Helyn inquired. There was no answer, but Miriam did not deny the fact. Her gaze stayed on me.

"Death seeks your soul, Adrian," she said. "He wants you to give it to him."

"How am I supposed to do that?" I asked. Miriam's expression wilted, like a flower that the sun scorched.

"Die," she answered.

"You mean," Alex said, "he'd have to let Death kill him." Miriam gave a slight nod. Helyn leaned closer to me and lowered her voice to a whisper.

"Adrian, I just heard something out there. We need to go now," she urgently demanded. Alex leapt to his feet.

"No, wait. I can't just leave her here," I protested.

"Well, we aren't going to carry Death's projection of your sister out of here," Alex argued. "Come on, stop talking with Death's confident and let's go."

"Stop talking about my sister that way!" I fired up, shoving myself to my feet.

"You two, quit it!" Helyn hissed. Alex raised his hands in surrender. I scowled. Helyn's brown eyes burned with passion and searched my face. "We have to go now...without her."

"Yes, go," Miriam pleaded. I glanced once more at the chains and then her beautiful features. Men shouted from outside the door. Helyn and Alex rushed out of the confined space. With a heavy heart, I tore myself away from Miriam and backed out of the tunnel.

I stood up and drew my sword at the scene that presented itself outside of Miriam's prison. Dozens of Death's men were on the attack, while Alex and Helyn tried to protect themselves. Nahum, Carissa, and others dropped into view and began to help. I gripped my sword tighter, but most of the fight had drained from me. Miriam wasn't alive. Why should I fight? Suddenly, something hit me hard from the side, and I fell to the ground. I looked up to find Death bending over me in disgust.

"You came to fight me, didn't you? Even after the offer to fight for your sister instead?"

"But she's just an illusion, a lure to bring me in. Besides, if you really wanted to help me, why didn't you restore my sister to me? Why do I have to fight you to get her?" I demanded.

"But you don't need to fight me," Death replied. "You need to fight yourself."

"Myself?"

"Let go of your need to wage war against everything and everyone. Give up, and she's yours," Death bargained. That sounded familiar. While the promise of having Miriam again was still appealing, I knew that 'give up' meant die. The thought of dying sent a cold shiver up my spine. I scowled and swung my sword over my head. Death backed up, and I leapt to my feet. I slashed at him again, and he grabbed my sword with his hand. It should have sliced through his palm, but nothing happened to him. Instead, he ripped the sword from my hands, throwing it across the room, and then struck me across the face.

Then, Death slammed the lower half of his body against my legs. They gave way, and I collapsed at his feet.

"Lord Jesus, save him!" Carissa cried out. Death's ice-blue eyes dimmed and turned to search the room. I scrambled to my feet, wondering at the low rumbling of the ground. A Faze Whip blade sliced through the air between myself and Death. The enemy took a step back.

"Adrian, let's go!" Nahum shouted. I ran for the exit, picking up the sword that Death had thrown earlier. The others broke from their fights, I helped Alex finish off his guy, and then we ran past the dark warriors and into the tunnels beyond.

"You're a fool, Adrian Falkner! The end of the Defense is near; you should be fighting for this side! My Phantom Warriors will destroy every last one of them, and I will destroy you!" Though he whispered the words, they had the effect of a shout. I groaned, shook my head, and ran on, at the lead of the flight from tunnels. Breathing heavily, we stepped into The Enclave what felt like an hour later. I looked back at the others. Helyn leaned over, hands on her knees, slowly catching her breath.

"Are you here to stay?" she posed. I wasn't sure how to answer. Now that Miriam could not be rescued, I didn't have a reason to stay. Although, a part of me still wanted to get even with Death for everything. Give up, he had said.

*Yeah, right. You're out to murder me! I'm supposed to fight that!*

Realizing that Helyn still waited for an answer, I silently shrugged. Helyn nodded and walked away. Everyone except Nahum and Carissa left. Carissa stepped up and grabbed my arm.

"Aren't you going to stay?" she invited in a soft, musical lilt. "Something special is happening tomorrow night. You'll want to see it."

"I don't know," I hesitated. Carissa narrowed her eyes.

"Not a curious guy, are you?" she wondered. Then, Carissa left, springing up into the nearest tree. I frowned.

"Oh, she did that on purpose," I muttered. Nahum looked after her and nodded subtly.

"Well, I'm ready to retire," he sighed. "Coming?" Nahum arched an eyebrow.

"Fine, you guys win. I'll stay for tomorrow night," I consented. After all, there was no reason to head back home where Mom would undoubtedly meet me with more questioning. Nahum flashed one of his rare smiles.

"Good."

+ + + + + + +

I couldn't sleep. Death's words seemed to hang over me like a lingering nightmare. *You're a fool, Adrian!*

I sighed, thinking over more of his words, for lack of anything better to do. Suddenly, I bolted up in bed.

"The tyrrohns!" I exclaimed. "Miriam said the tyrrohns are Phantom Warriors!"

"You're just now figuring that out?" Nahum asked, rolling over on his cot, his voice hoarse.

"Hey! You said the Ruling Heads sent them." I jumped up from my bed.

"We thought they were until you came along." Nahum rolled back over and pulled the covers over his face.

"What do you mean, 'until I came along'?" I growled, wondering if he was blaming me for the discovery.

"We didn't know Death until you came, how could we know who his men were?" Nahum posed rhetorically, his face still under the covers.

"But when did you know? Why didn't you tell me? Come on, Nahum!" I urged.

"Oh, Adrian, really? You want to do this now?" Nahum groaned, rolling back over to face me and throwing the covers off his face. "Alright, fine. The tyrrohns are Phantom Warriors. Now, go back to sleep." Nahum buried himself under the covers again. I reasoned that Nahum had probably worked all day and now into the night because of me, so he ought to be allowed to sleep. I crawled back into my cot, hoping sleep would come soon.

+ + + + + + +

The Enclave came alive the next evening with every man, woman, and child moving at the same time toward a common goal. I watched the Defenders walk past my tent in family units, the children laughing, talking, and singing. Some walked in pairs, speaking to each other with smiles and great animation. I finally dragged myself out to discover what their destination was.

"Are you coming with us?" Carissa asked as she walked past. I jogged to catch up with her.

"Where are you going?" I asked.

"Didn't I say something special was happening tonight?" Carissa posed. I nodded.

"Is it happening outside The Enclave?" I wondered.

"No, at our Center. Helyn did tell you that there are seven Centers, right?" Carissa replied.

"No. One for each, uh, group, right?" I guessed.

"Yes, one for each kinship," Carissa affirmed. "The Center is the only place large enough to hold all the families from each kinship, and even then we spill into the surrounding forest, sitting and standing in groups. Like a family gathering of large proportion!"

"So, what's the occasion?"

"An Ezra assembly," Carissa answered. I stared at her uncomprehendingly. Carissa continued, "When the kinship is assembled, the leader will read from the Scriptures."

"Don't you do that every day?" I asked. Carissa smiled.

"Sure, but this is different," was her mysteriously reply.

"Come on, Carissa, spill it," I urged.

"Titus is a very busy man, being one of the seven leaders, but I love to hear him speak. He's…like a gentle father, speaking to you in a way you'll understand, without patronizing you. He just makes you want to listen," Carissa explained.

"Are you not going to answer my question?" I persisted. She appeared to ignore me, and picked up where she'd left off as we continued walking.

"Titus usually speaks only to his kinship. He says that's where his duty lies. Sometimes, I wish I could have been born into Titus' kinship," Carissa laughed. "About once every year, Titus is persuaded to speak to the other kinships. Tonight, he's speaking to ours." Carissa's green eyes sparkled. My brow furrowed.

"You mean, you convinced me to stay to hear a Defense leader speak?" I posed.

"Perhaps," Carissa nodded. I whirled around to leave, but Carissa grabbed my arm. "Wait until you hear him, Adrian."

"What is so important about this?" I queried.

"You'll have to tell me…when you've heard Titus speak," Carissa challenged. Her eyes held mine steadily.

After a moment of silence, I huffed and gave in. We walked on until we reached the Center. As Carissa had said it would be, the place was overflowing with Defenders. They were all talking in a voice as low as a hum.

They weren't communicating with each other. Instead, I had the feeling they were praying. Among them, I saw Helyn and Nahum. Carissa pointed out the leader, Titus. He stood a head above all the other Defenders.

"After the apostles had received the gift of the Holy Spirit, they began to preach to the people," Titus was saying. "They proclaimed the truth of Jesus Christ, how He had been handed over to be killed, even though He had been perfect. They preached with power and truth, and every man understood what was being spoken by the apostle Peter when he said, 'Therefore let all Israel be assured of this: God has made this Jesus, whom you crucified, both Lord and Christ.

When the people heard this, they were cut to the heart and said to Peter and the other apostles, 'Brothers, what shall we do?'

Peter said, 'Repent and be baptized, every one of you, in the name of Jesus Christ for the forgiveness of your sins. And you will receive the gift of the Holy Spirit. The promise is for you and your children and for all who are far off – for all whom the Lord our God will call.'"

The whole assembly cried out, "amen!" Even if I wanted to pry myself away from the religious teachings, I couldn't have. Titus' glowing face and clear voice held me in place.

"It is as the apostle Paul wrote in his letter," Titus quoted. "'If you confess with your mouth, "Jesus is Lord," and believe in your heart that God raised him from the dead, you will be saved.' Saved from sin. Oh, the glorious thought that Jesus' sacrifice takes away our sin and its penalty...if we only believe." Titus stretched out his hands as if embracing the crowd around him. My heart skipped a beat.

*Take away our sin and the penalty*, I mentally repeated. *You mean, that Christ would take away the thievery I did and the title of 'tyrrohn ally?' Would it, then, still be my fault that Miriam died?*

Carissa moved forward.

"Are you going to join us?" she whispered. I shook my head.

"I'll just stay here," I replied. Carissa nodded.

"By the way," she added, "Naric heard of your arrival. He asked if you would meet him in the Tent of Meetings later."

"Uh...sure," I nodded.

"Great. I'll take you after this." Carissa left, and I sat crisscross-applesauce on the grass. The Defenders had ceased praying and were talking to each other. The children were playing with various items. Two young boys had picked up wooden swords to enact a fight. Carissa joined the group as if she had been there the whole time. Helyn embraced her, and the two spoke animatedly. When Titus began to speak again, the whole assembly quieted, even the children, and listened to him. Choruses of "amen," cheers, and the hum of praying would follow his short, captivating speeches. Then, everyone would begin talking or playing again. While the Defenders around him spoke, laughed, and played, Titus remained nearly unmoved. He had a Bible in one hand, and his gaze went continually upward. Titus' smile never wavered, and when Defenders spoke to him, his joy seemed to display itself on the other's face. Several children ran up to him once and he knelt on their level to speak with them. The service seemed to have no end, yet I found myself too interested to leave.

"Hey!" Alex called. I flinched, and my head snapped around to find him weaving through tents to join me.

"Hey, yourself. Where have you been all day?" I inquired.

"Training in another Center. Colin told me I'd find you here," Alex answered. "So, what are you doing?" he asked, plopping on the ground.

"Uh, watching," I answered.

"I don't understand it." Alex motioned toward the crowd. "We know Death is out there, and they're talking like it's all a party. I keep wondering if Death's gonna leap out from somewhere." I brought my knees up to my chest and pondered what he had just said.

Words that Naric had spoken to me before rose to the front of my mind.

*Where, O death, is thy sting?* I thought. Obviously, his presence and purpose did not sting the Defenders. For me, on the other hand, everything about Death hurt.

+++++++

Carissa showed me the way to the Tent of Meetings late that night. I entered alone. Naric and Colin stood talking to each other in low tones. Naric looked up and motioned me to come.

"Welcome, Adrian. I was hoping you'd return," he greeted.

"After all, who else would I shoot at?" Colin joked. I smirked, and Colin faked a cough to cover his laugh. "All right. Down to business. Nahum told me you all took a little...mission last night."

"Yeah. It didn't quite go as planned," I said.

"What was planned?" Naric wondered. I scowled. How was I supposed to answer that question? Suddenly, the tent flap flew open, and Helyn rushed in.

"Command...oh. Uh, sorry." She went for a quick retreat.

"No, it's alright, Helyn," Naric assured her. "Come in and speak." Helyn came back inside the tent. She flashed me a look, which carried an unspoken emotion.

"I'm, uh, heading home in the morning. Is it alright if I take all five horses with me this time?" Helyn requested.

"Of course," Naric nodded.

"Thanks."

"A moment more of your time, please, Helyn," Naric began. "Were you a part of the mission last night?"

"Yes, sir," she nodded. Again, she flashed a look toward me. A fire kindled inside of me. Was Naric going to ask Helyn instead of letting me answer for myself?

"What was your team headed to the Underground for?" the commander queried. Helyn looked at me and raised her eyebrows. She was letting me answer.

"Attempting a rescue of Miriam," I boldly answered.

"Your sister?" Colin clarified. I nodded. "I'm sorry it didn't work. What happened?"

"Well...um, Death had too many...Phantom Warriors...for us to handle," I stammered.

"Phantom Warriors? What are those?" Colin blurted out.

"His soldiers," Helyn replied. "Death called them such." Naric and Colin exchanged glances.

"You know," I began, "If we mounted a larger group, we could easily overtake Death."

"To end him, right?" Helyn turned to me. Her brown eyes were piercing. The resolve inside to get back at Death for haunting me with Miriam's beautiful face sparked anew. I nodded slowly.

"Undoubtedly."

"Now, hold on, you two," Naric cut in. "This isn't much of a battle plan."

"It's simple," I countered. "Last night, Death said that the end of the Defense is near, which means he's planning an attack soon."

"I must be missing something," Colin stated.

"Death won't be coming with his men. He wants to kill me by singling me out, and he won't risk the chance of getting killed by another Defender. So, while the attack is happening, some of us sneak away and defeat Death," I decided.

"That might just work," Naric nodded. "He knows Adrian is with us. We should evacuate the women and children to the Fort. If need be, we can even fall back there to fight."

"Perhaps we set a trap," Helyn put in. "Lead them to the Fort on purpose. After all, their numbers are stronger than ours."

"I like the way you think, Miss Helyn," Colin grinned.

"But why evacuate and put up a trap at all? Why risk the Phantom Warriors outsmarting us?" I pointed out. "Why not attack right now? Look." I crossed the room and pointed to the map of the Underground, which was laid on the short table. "Send the Defenders through these tunnels. Death will know and send his men to attack you. While his men are gone, some of us can defeat Death," I detailed.

"Well, I like your confidence, Adrian," Colin spoke. Naric picked up.

"The decision will have to be brought before the other leaders. We must seek counsel. It would be better to make sure we are ready, and the women and children are safe," he said. I frowned. Helyn stepped forward.

"Adrian, he's right," she said.

"I thought you said I was supposed to defeat Death," I argued. Helyn arched an eyebrow.

"You're angry at Death," she said matter-of-factly.

"I have every right to be," I growled.

"You will defeat Death, Adrian, but not in anger. And not alone. It's best to wait," Helyn maintained.

My frown deepened, and I clenched my fists.

"You wait!" I shouted at them. "Waiting is cowardly!" I turned and stormed out of the tent.

*They don't care, Adrian. They act like they care, but they're just lying to you! So, do it without them! Get down there and kill him! Rid yourself of that stupid, undeserved title without their help! It's not about them anyway!*

"Adrian, stop!" Naric's voice called. I ran faster, darting between tents and dodging the Defenders on patrol. Naric followed, calling after me every so often. I hurried past a family singing in their tent, the long fire pits from which the women served meals, and then around the next row of tents. I was almost there.

Naric's boots pounded noisily on the ground as he kept close enough. Up ahead, the Center's entrance was guarded by three or four armed men.

"Grab him!" Naric shouted. I attempted to leap over the ropes which separated the Center from the rest of The Enclave, but one of the Defenders grabbed my arm.

"Let go of me!" I screamed, pulling with all my might.

"Calm down," the man said slowly. Naric ran up, slightly out of breath, but with a look of determination on his face that I had never seen before.

"Adrian, I know what you're thinking, and I can't allow you to do that," Naric said firmly.

"Why not? He's tortured every night with the face of my brother, and every day with the memory of my sister! I'm done with this! He's dying," I argued, wrenching my arm out of the Defender's grasp.

"I'm not denying the struggles that Death has caused you, Adrian, but you'll be killed if you go alone," Naric contended.

"As if you'd care," I growled, taking several steps back. Naric closed the distance between us.

"I'm sorry you feel that way, but I'm trying to protect you," he said. I clenched my fists and bit back my retort. Naric added, "I'm sure your father would be doing the same thing."

"Yeah, and I'd hate him for it!" I shouted. Then, I turned and sprinted into the Center, grabbed the nearest weapon, and took off into the woods. Naric didn't follow.

# CHAPTER ELEVEN

## The Lamb's Blood

Armed with a Faze Whip, I entered the tunnels of the Underground again. Trying to be quiet, I moved through the tunnels, just waiting for Death to show himself. I had it all planned out in my head. Death would appear, and then I would slash out with the Faze Whip, running a blade straight through his heart. It would be easy. I stopped as soon as I got to the empty room where I had found the door to Miriam's prison. I had expected to find him there, though I wasn't sure why. Moving into the middle of the room slowly and turning around, I eyed the place carefully.

"You came back again?" Death's voice was followed by his laugh. I heard him drop behind me but didn't have enough time to move before he hit me, tossing me to the floor. "Finally, Adrian Falkner came alone. Now I can finish you once and for all."

I acknowledged the challenge this time and rose, preparing my weapon. Going over the move once more in my head, I leapt at Death and swung the Faze Whip at him. He used his arms to shield himself and push me back again. He ran at me, vaulting over my head at the last second. I turned around to face him and struck out as soon as his feet hit the ground.

He again raised an arm to block the blow. Then, I swung down at him, and he grabbed my weapon. I managed to hold on. Death twisted the Faze Whip and lifted it over my head, so my arms came painfully behind me. I let go of the weapon and instinctively dropped as he swung above me. Rolling to my left, I barely avoided getting a blade in my back.

I jumped up to face Death, but he twirled the weapon quickly, forcing me to step backward until my back pressed against a wall. I leapt to the right, and the wall took the intended blow. The Faze Whip stuck in the compacted dirt, and Death made no move to get it out. Instead, he pursued me as I tried to put distance between us. For barely a moment, we stood at a face-off. Then, Death threw his hands toward me, and it took me little to no time to figure out that he was throwing daggers. I jumped, fell to the floor, and leaned every which way to dodge them.

One sliced through my pants and into my left leg, another grazed my right arm. I closed the distance between us. Death kicked me in the stomach forcefully, and I fell back a few steps. He came at me, swinging his arms like battle axes. I ducked to avoid them and dropped on my back. He raised a foot to pin me down, but I rolled and stood back up behind him.

Death whirled around, and his arm plowed into my head. I was sent flying backward and into a wall. Death came to stand over me and pressed his foot on my chest. I gasped for breath.

Above me, there was the faint outline of a Faze Whip. I frowned in determination and grabbed the Faze Whip. Jerking it from the wall, I made one of the blades strike Death's face. I spun the Faze Whip to make the other blade also slice across his face. He fell backward with a groan, and I quickly got away from the wall.

Death looked up, his face more horrid looking than ever. His eyes flashed brightly. He ran at me and jumped high in the air. I backed up to avoid being landed on. Death landed, and the ground shook. Barely keeping my footing, I tried to dodge two of his daggers and then prepare for his oncoming attack. One knife missed, another grazed my face. I didn't have enough time to prepare for Death's next move, and his punch landed square in my chest. The air was knocked out of me, and somehow my weak attempt to block Death's next blow worked.

I couldn't gain any air. I gave him another whack in the face. Death grabbed my weapon and began to twist it from my grasp. I still hadn't gotten any oxygen. My grip began to weaken, and my mind started spinning. I let go of the weapon and fell to the ground to avoid his hit. I choked and tried hard to calm myself and breathe. Death kicked me in the stomach, and I started to blackout. I crawled away from him, but couldn't pick myself up.

Finally, I was able to take deep, gasping breaths. I didn't get enough time before I saw Death come and use my Faze Whip to hit me. I wasn't sure exactly where the weapon hit; everything stung. Then, Death grabbed me, lifting me above the ground and slamming my body against the nearest wall. My body hit with a resounding smack and then crumbled to the ground when he let go. I glanced up at Death, only noticing how his ice blue eyes gleamed with satisfaction.

I struggled for another deep breath. Intense pain shot up my back, pounded in my head, and cramped my stomach. My chest hurt from lack of air. I felt blood trickle down the side of my face, and my leg continued to throb from the wound. I could barely see Death's figure anymore; my vision was hazy and wobbly. Death's words resonated in my head, though I could feel his breath on my ear.

"Why have you fought so hard? Did you honestly think your soul could be saved? Did you believe the lies those fools told you?" Death whispered. My body shook violently, and my eyes clenched shut. Why was he patronizing me? Why not just hurry up and kill me?

Death continued, "Did you believe the words of the Scriptures could save your soul? Answer me, Adrian Falkner!"

"I don't know," I gasped out. Death slammed my shoulder, sending pain down my spine and all the way to my toes.

"Tell me," he whispered, coming even closer. "Can their God save you?"

"Are you…talking about…Je–"

"Silence!" Death struck me again. This time, the pain jerked my senses back into function for a minute, and I opened my eyes again. The enemy's ice-blue eyes piercingly flooded my vision. His black form was but a blur. The longer I stared, the brighter his eyes became. "Give only the answer to this: can their God save you?" Death persisted. I wanted a good comeback, a bold answer, something to knock him off his game, but only one thing came to mind: Titus' words.

*'If you confess with your mouth, "Jesus is Lord," and believe in your heart that God raised him from the dead, you will be saved.'*

It sounded like a surety. Except I didn't believe it, so how could I ward off Death with such an answer?

"Will you not answer?" Death hissed, grabbing my shirt and jerking me to my feet. "Fine! I will. He cannot save you, he is nothing but a fable. Your soul is mine!"

"My soul..." I choked out, clenching my eyes against the brilliance of his eyes and the pain which vibrated through my body. "My soul belongs to me." With a guttural snarl, Death shoved me back to the ground. The extra jolt caused the loss of every sense, darkness and silence enveloped me.

+ + + + + + +

I heard a groan, felt my body moving, and my eyes blinked open, but it all seemed a dream. Everything was black. A breathless silence hung in the dank air which only my rasping breaths broke. Various aches and pain gradually brought my senses to further alertness, but I struggled to recall what had caused the bleeding and throbbing. A haunting voice rang in my head, persistently crying "can he save you? Can he save you?" I turned my head, sending a stab down my spine, trying to get away from Death's whisper.

"I don't know if he can," I murmured. "Titus said he could, Death said he can't. Stop asking, please. I don't know." Slowly, cautiously, I decided to move and got as far as my knees before the world tilted and I groped for support in the darkness. My hands found a solid wall and I gladly leaned against it, finding little relief from the discomfort. Then, the battle with Death came back with some clarity.

"My soul," I repeated, "belongs to me. Who else has the right to own it? Maybe...my Creator?" The thought, spoken aloud, caused me to jerk upright. Weeks ago, Naric had spoken that foremost belief of the Defense: God is the Creator.

"But," I called out, as if speaking to someone invisible, "but just because He created me doesn't mean I have to give Him my soul. But, Adrian, isn't that what He came to save? Men's souls? Oh, is that what Death meant? Can Jesus Christ save my soul? Well, Titus said He could. If you confess that Jesus is

Lord..." My own words stopped me. It felt as though I was not truly speaking, but Someone was speaking to me through myself. I slouched against the cool, dirt wall again. At last, it all made sense.

"If Jesus is Lord, then, yes, He can save my soul. My soul doesn't belong to me. It belongs to Him." The moment these words had come out of my mouth, I got into a kneeling position. Truth had finally hit home. Jesus needed to be my Lord...today.

+++++++

After a few minutes of prayer, my body gave out again. I sank into the deepest of dreams. All of a sudden, a peculiar shuffling sound made me turn my head. Then, from the depth of the shadows, Miriam emerged.

"Miriam!" I cried out and reached for her. The motion felt slow and abnormal. Miriam drew closer, tears streaming down her cheeks.

"I heard everything," she whispered.

"I don't get it," I wheezed out, shifting my weary body. "Why didn't Death just kill me?"

"Because he couldn't. The Lord Almighty has plans for you, brother, and until His plans are fulfilled, you're not going anywhere," Miriam beamingly replied. Tears filled my eyes.

"Can I still not save you?" I moaned. Miriam's answer was to step away and disappear back into the darkness. I called after her, but she did not return. Things grew fuzzy. I realized after a minute that my eyes were closed. I made an effort to open my eyes and failed. Sometime later, I opened my eyes and struggled to move to a more comfortable position. Still, my body would not move. Voices seemed to drift into the prison from outside; deep, male voices that were speaking in quiet, urgent tones. I figured it was part of another strange dream connected to my pain.

"Adrian!" The voice was piercingly clear and familiar. "I found him!" There was a general scuttle and more voices. Their voices were a warbling sound like one speaking underwater. I had the feeling that I was being lifted upward, and my stomach dropped. Finally, my senses left me entirely unconscious.

+++++++

I opened my eyes and was astounded to find that I could move my body. Light flooded my vision, harshly stinging my eyes. I lifted a hand to wipe the salty liquid that obstructed my eyesight, then raised my head to look around. I was in Nahum's tent on the soft fur bed. Nahum himself sat on the bed opposite me, running a stone along the edge of a Faze Whip blade.

"What happened?" My voice came out as a hoarse, choking sound. Nahum looked up and set the Faze Whip aside.

"Welcome back to the land of the living," he quipped. I attempted to sit up, willing to test how much my body would move, but Nahum pushed me back down.

"Easy, Adrian. You have quite a few nasty wounds. It's best not to move until the doctor says you can."

"What doctor?" I rasped out.

"Well, in this case, I think Commander Naric is in charge."

"So, what happened?"

"I don't know. You're going to have to tell us. I came back from scouting, after Titus' talk, and Naric said you'd left in a storm. I got a little rest and woke up before dawn. You hadn't returned. So, I took a team and went down to find you. By the way, this yours?" Nahum turned and picked up a small wooden cross. The chain was no longer attached, but I recognized it right away.

"Yeah."

"We found it outside the room where we found you. Well, something akin to you," Nahum muttered. I winced.

"Nahum!" Naric's voice proceeded him. He stormed into the tent with Alex behind him. "I thought I told you to inform me immediately when he woke up."

"Yes, sir, but Adrian needed to be told to stay down. Besides, Alex was already on his way," Nahum returned.

"How does he know this stuff?" Alex gasped. Naric shook his head, and his gaze turned to me.

"How are you feeling, Adrian?"

"Horrible," I grimaced. Naric scoffed under his breath.

"Well, you should. Alex, go back to the Tent of Meetings and ask for Howard. Nahum, the team is waiting for a report on Adrian's condition." It was apparent that Naric wanted to speak with me alone. Alex and Nahum left. "Here, I brought something to help with your pain." I swallowed what I was told to and laid back again. Naric took a seat on Nahum's pallet.

"I'm sure you have quite the story to tell," he began. "I'd be interested to hear it." I looked at the cross and smiled. I stared at the cross most of the time as I related my story. Naric listened silently. When I had finished, the joy of knowing I was saved from sin had returned in full measure.

"You know," Naric commented, "that symbol will always bring you back to where you need to be." His eyes were on the object in my hand.

"The cross?" I clarified.

"Indeed. Because it was on a cross that Jesus Christ died to save men's souls." Naric rose with a smile. "You need to rest now. I'm glad to have you back, my brother-in-Christ, and to be able to fight by your side in this battle later," Naric said as he exited the tent. I sank into the warmth and comfort of the bed.

Looking at the cross once more, I whispered, "He can save my soul. He did."

# CHAPTER TWELVE

## Tongues of Fire

Naric personally oversaw my recovery and encouraged me in my newfound faith. He often came to stand or sit by my beside, talking and reading Scripture. One of the things we talked about was his challenge to me. Know who you are and by what means you stand. I knew who I was, a sinner, and the means by which I had stood was my pride. I knew now that I was redeemed, and the means by which I stood was all in Christ.

My recovery was slow. I was on bed-rest for a full week because of a concussion. Even after I was allowed to rise from the bed and leave the tent, Naric strictly forbade any training outside the Scriptures. I think Nahum chaffed at the slow recovery as much as myself. One day, he took me to walk around The Enclave perimeter.

"We've got to speed up the recovery of your leg," he commented.

"I agree, but what is the walking doing for me exactly?" I asked, limping alongside him.

"Getting you on your feet, for one thing," Nahum replied.

"Yeah, Alex says I'm 'absolutely lazy.'" As Nahum and I walked, our attention was continually drawn to goings on in The Enclave. There was never a dull moment. This home for thousands of families was alive with hundreds of activities every day. On this walk, it struck me how close all these families had to be to live in tents every single day.

"Dad and I would kill each other," I mumbled a thought aloud. Nahum's eyebrows raised in surprise.

"If?" he prodded. The question hung in the air as I considered answering it.

"If," I finally decided to say, "we lived so close to each other all the time."

"I think you'd find you have more in common than you think," Nahum swiftly replied. "And common ground builds relationships."

"You don't know my dad," I argued.

"It sounds like you don't know him either," Nahum quietly stated. My face flushed, but I bit my tongue. Nahum's countenance had dropped significantly, and I was reminded that he had lost his parents. Our conversation lagged and then stopped entirely. We walked on until we reached the horses' pen. Nahum leaned over the fence to pet one of them. I cleared my throat. It was time to speak again.

"I've, uh, been meaning to tell you, Nahum…well, I'm sorry."

Nahum glanced at me. "For what?"

"Being a horrible friend. Thinking only of myself and my own problems," I clarified. Nahum pulled his arm back over the fence.

"Thanks. I forgive you, Adrian," he said. "You know, you're even closer than a friend now, anyway."

"What do you mean?" I asked. Nahum started walking again.

"You're a brother-in-Christ. We're all brothers and sisters in Christ. That's why our units are called kinships," he explained.

"I like that," I said. However, the thought of my only brother, Morro, cast a shadow on the idea.

+ + + + + + +

A few days later, I went to the Tent of Meetings. Since being allowed up, Naric had required me to meet him or the doctor-leader, Howard, for 'analysis and therapy.' In other words, they were just keeping a close eye on my every move. If I didn't show up, one of them found me.

Since I didn't have anything else to fill my time, I decided a walk to the Tent of Meetings would be good for me today. I pushed the tent flap aside and limped in. All the leaders were present.

"Ah, Adrian," Naric smiled. "Please, come in. We were just starting our meeting."

"I can wait..."

"No, they want to hear your story," Naric said. He motioned to a seat next to him. I hesitated a moment, then took the place. I tentatively told my story, and every leader listened with interest in the details.

Once finished, Colin was the first to speak up. "And to think I doubted the Lord's plan," he said. "All this time, He was preparing you for this defeat and victory. Huh." His words sparked a memory that I couldn't quite place. Howard, the leader and doctor, stood from his chair.

"How's the arm healing?" he wondered, crossing over to me.

"Fine," I shrugged.

"The leg?"

"Well, I won't be running anywhere without being threatened," I quipped.

"Think you could handle a little sword training?" Robert asked hopefully, glancing between Naric and Howard.

"I don't see why not," Howard nodded.

"Please, not the wooden one," I pleaded. The leaders laughed.

"No promises," Robert winked.

"What about my part?" Colin wondered. "Honestly, I'd like to get to shoot at you again."

"Uh, bad leg. Did you hear that one?" I protested. More laughter.

"Fair enough," Colin exclaimed, raising his hands in defeat. Naric stood.

"I don't have any problem with Adrian getting back into the training, but let's keep it simple and short." He looked directly at Robert. Robert nodded.

"Now," Naric said, "to the task at hand. What are our strategies against Death?"

"Evacuating women and children to the Fort for safety, doubling the scouts, and perhaps setting a trap to lure the Phantom Warriors in certain directions," I suggested. "While most of the Defenders fight off the Phantom Warriors, I take several others and go after Death, who will be alone."

"Not a bad plan," Colin joked. For some reason, I couldn't smile back. The unknown gnawed at me bitterly. Naric noticed my unenthusiastic response.

"What's wrong?" he asked.

"Well, it's just…I couldn't take Death last time when he was alone. He defeated me without having to call his men. So, what good will it do to try again, even with the others?" I pondered aloud.

"Adrian, when you went to fight Death the last time had you accepted the quest given to you?" Naric posed.

"Uh, I've forgotten the quest," I admitted, rather ashamedly.

"You're looking this quest straight in the face. You were called to defeat Death. To complete the task, though, you had to allow yourself to change. You have done so by believing in Jesus' name and accepting Him as your Lord. All you need now is to finish it.

Who says the Lord will not give you the victory?" Naric posed. I frowned.

*Victory? Belief? Called? Why are those words so familiar?*

+++++++

I sat in the Center, resting from my training earlier and watching people pass and drill around me. I took another drink from the cup in my hand. Out of the corner of my eye, I caught sight of familiar faces. I dropped the cup and left my sword leaning against the log.

"Helyn, Nahum! Wait up!" I called after them. They turned and waited as I limped up to them.

"You're looking better," Nahum commented, gesturing toward me with his Faze Whip. Helyn winced.

"Yeah, every muscle in my body hurts right now, but I'm good. Reminds me of Ledo practice," I chuckled. Nahum smirked.

"How'd the sword-play go?" he asked.

"Pretty good," I nodded, glancing at Helyn. She had taken a step back and was looking at the ground.

"So, Faze Whip training tomorrow instead?" Nahum invited.

"Yeah! Oh. I don't have my Faze Whip anymore," I mentioned.

"You think I picked up the cross without taking the Faze Whip, Adrian? Come on. I've got it," Nahum said. I grinned.

"Do you use a Faze Whip, Helyn?" I attempted to bring her into the conversation. Helyn lifted her head and shook it.

"Nahum's never let me touch one before," she said. Nahum frowned.

"I did, too. Didn't I?" He looked at her questioningly. Helyn smiled and shook her head again.

"No, you didn't," she answered slowly.

"So, you'll join us tomorrow?" Nahum asked, giving his Faze Whip a twirl. Helyn glanced at me.

"Maybe not," she declined. Nahum shrugged.

"Your call." He spun around and walked away, while Helyn stayed a moment longer. I shifted my weight.

"I'm, uh…I'm here to stay," I began. Helyn nodded.

"Nahum was telling me."

"So, what's wrong? I mean…you're just so… cheery…you know, usually…and right now, you're… not," I finished lamely. Helyn took a deep breath.

"It hurt, Adrian," she said. I frowned.

"What did?" As soon as I had asked the question, I knew it was a stupid one.

Helyn turned and called back over her shoulder, "That you wouldn't listen. That you thought we didn't care. That you left."

+ + + + + + +

I limped hurriedly out of the Center the next day, my Faze Whip already in my hand. Nahum had told me where to meet him. I took one glance back at The Enclave on my way into the woods. Despite the waiting around for Death to attack, the packing and planning to move the women and children to the Fort, and long hours of vigilant scouting, the Defenders had been relatively calm. Nothing was nervous or tense about these people.

The first group of women and children were leaving today, but instead of the crying I had expected, everything was done with smiles and excitement. At last, I spotted the three large elm trees that Nahum had described. They formed a lopsided triangle. I figured he was already waiting for me.

Suddenly, something thudded behind me. I turned to see what had happened, but before I saw anything, everything went black. I kicked against the attacker, making my injured leg cry out in protest. Swinging my left hand around, I expected to feel the balanced weight of the Faze Whip. Instead, my hand grazed through the open air. It had been taken from me! As I struggled, my attacker pulled me backward.

"Attack me fairly, Death!" I screamed. The grip on my arms tightened. Twisting and pulling was useless. With a grunt, my attacker shoved me to the ground, sitting upright. Quick as lighting, a metal clamp snapped shut around my left hand.

"No!" I jerked my right hand just in time for the clamp to miss. I limped forward. *Thump.* "Aah!" I screamed at the tree trunk I had run in to. I veered right, and then the chain on my left hand grew taunt.

"Hey! Adrian, we're attached!" a voice cried out.

"Helyn?" Then, the second clamp was closed around my right wrist, and I was dragged backward again. "Come on, take off the hood and..." Someone lifted the hood quickly, and I glanced around for signs of the attacker. The deep woods of Chahcan surrounded me; old trees with low-hung branches which grey and green moss covered like blankets. Helyn's right hand was attached to my left, and her left hand was connected to a chain that wrapped around a tree. Nahum was on my right, similarly situated.

"What is going on?" I asked.

"I don't know," Nahum said. "My hood just came off, too. I was waiting for you, and then someone knocked me out of the tree from behind."

"Death?" I inquired.

"Not entirely improbable," Nahum agreed. "What do you think, Helyn?"

"Don't look at me. I wasn't even coming out here for Faze Whip training and somehow got roped into this anyway," Helyn shot back. Nahum tilted his head and scanned the trees above us.

"Unless we're a lure, something about this approach doesn't seem like Death," he stated.

"So, Phantom Warriors?" I guessed.

"They would have run us through," Nahum replied.

"So, what are you saying, Nahum?" Helyn questioned. Nahum shrugged noisily, jostling the chains on his arms.

"I thought we weren't supposed to be talking to you," he said. Helyn huffed.

"Well, I just didn't think Adrian would care to," she retorted. I sighed.

"That's weird," Nahum commented. "Adrian, weren't you just telling me last night that you needed to tell Helyn something?" His look prompted me to speak, but Helyn's look made it awkward.

"Yeah, uh…Helyn, I'm sorry…for hurting you," I stammered. Helyn's expression wavered between a smile and puzzlement.

"You're apologizing?" she wondered, tilting her head.

"I was wrong. I know that now," I blurted out. My gaze kept darting around the forest, looking for signs of the one who had chained us. Nonetheless, I saw Helyn scoot as close as she could and draw her knees toward her chest.

"I sense a story," she said. Nahum looked up into the trees again.

"I don't see or hear Death or his men around us. If they are around, we've a short time before they show up again," he mentioned.

"So, we should get out before Adrian tells his story," Helyn summarized.

"That depends," Nahum said.

"Depends on what?" I queried.

"On how fast you can tell a story," he smirked. Helyn and I laughed. It was so strange, being chained to trees in the forest with Death or his men coming for us and laughing at the same time.

"I'm pretty quick, but if Phantom Warriors are coming, I'd rather have my Faze Whip back," I said.

"Same," Nahum agreed.

"So, is this an 'I-know-how-to-get-out-of-the-chains' kind of situation," Helyn began, "or is this an 'I'm-trying-to-be-confident-even-though-I-have-no-idea-how-to-get-out-of-the-chains' kind of situation?" I frowned.

"Um, the first one? Because it sounded better?"

"Adrian Falkner," a new voice cut in. "You are definitely the second one." A slim, girlish figure swung down from the trees with two Faze Whips in her hands. "Luckily, I found a key." She put down the Faze Whips and drew out a tiny, silver object.

"Carissa, you're amazing!" Helyn cheered.

"Okay, hurry up," Nahum urged. Carissa unlocked Helyn first, me second, and Nahum last. As the lock released, Carissa put on a smug smile.

"So, now is probably not a good time to tell you that I'm the one who chained you up, is it?" she asked.

"Carissa Harris!" I protested.

"Why, you little...!" Nahum leapt toward her. Carissa spun away and ran through the forest, laughing. Nahum gave chase, and the two ran, twisted, and ducked through the forestry. Helyn and I looked on laughingly. When they disappeared from sight, I bent and picked up the Faze Whips.

"Since the enemy isn't around, how about a Faze Whip lesson?" I extended Nahum's Whip toward Helyn. Her brown eyes widened.

"Would he let me?"

"About time he did."

"What about your story?" Helyn asked.

"We'll get to it," I promised. Nahum returned a minute later, out of breath from his run, and took over my attempted lesson. He wouldn't tell us what had happened to Carissa, but I sensed that she had gotten away from him. Helyn and I were in the middle of learning how to fight each other when another voice shouted over Nahum's instructions.

"What are you doing?" I looked past Nahum and found Alex running up. While I was distracted, Helyn knocked me down.

"Gotcha," she declared playfully.

"So not fair," I told her. Helyn offered her hand, and I used my good leg to steady myself again. Alex approached cautiously.

"Are you going to hit me with that thing, too?" he asked, pointing at the Faze Whip in Helyn's hands. She hefted it in her hands and eyed him.

"I might," she considered.

"Yeah, do it!" I cheered.

"Hey! At least, give me yours like a good friend," Alex protested.

"Okay." I tossed him the weapon. "And good luck."

+ + + + + + +

Storytelling waited until the end of the day when I was exhausted, and Helyn dragged me from the Tent of Meetings to the horses' pen. We sat alone on a fallen log. Helyn pulled one knee toward her chest and wrapped her hands around it.

"Okay. Go." I smiled and began. Throughout the whole story, Helyn didn't say a word. I could tell she was making an effort to get past the pain I had caused her and rejoice. By the end of the story, Helyn was grinning like the first time I had met her.

"Welcome to the family of God," she said. "By the way, your apology is accepted."

"Thanks." I gave her a flicker of a smile, then sighed.

"What's wrong?" Helyn asked.

"I just thought...I'd finally get Miriam back. She'd bring our family back together...like it had been. Now, it will never be possible."

"I know you'd like to think she would bring your family together like it's always been, but…Adrian Falkner, three years changes things. You're not the same," Helyn said softly. "Miriam can no longer hold your family together."

"So, Jesus can?" I posed. Helyn nodded slowly, but I shook my head. "You know, I don't get it. 'Where, O death, is your sting?' That doesn't make sense to me, even now. It still stings." Helyn smiled.

"Death does hurt Christians, Adrian…just not the same way. We do not grieve as the world grieves because we have hope. All who believe in Jesus' name will go to heaven when they die, and we who also believe in Jesus' name have the hope of meeting them one day. Since you have believed, you may also have this hope, Adrian," Helyn explained gently.

"Do you think…is Miriam in heaven?" I asked her. Helyn knit her brow slightly, but a smile graced her lips.

"I don't know for certain, but I will pray that the Prince of Peace will comfort you no matter the circumstances of the past, present, or future," she promised quietly.

"Thanks, Helyn."

"Anytime," Helyn assured me. "I was wondering, have you read any more of Fighters from Ancient Days?"

"No, why?"

"Because the next one might make sense to you now. It says, 'But released from your fears, a new Power will take hold, and the One who holds the key will shut the Gates of Suffering, so that you may not enter.'" I pondered this silently for a minute, then looked at her with furrowed brow.

"That's supposed to mean something to me?"

"Oh, come on, you've got this. Remember how the first lines meant that we were already dead in sin," Helyn prodded.

"Right, so...this is about coming back to life?" I asked.

"I'll give you one more hint. First Corinthians 15:22 says, 'for as in Adam all die, so in Christ all will be made alive.'"

"Oh. So, Jesus Christ is the one who holds the key to the Gates of Suffering," I exclaimed. Helyn nodded eagerly. "But, why can I not enter?"

A new voice suddenly chimed in, "is he always this slow?" Nahum dropped from one of the trees and Helyn backhanded him, slapping his side.

"Hush, you! He's getting it," she scolded. Pursing my lips together so my thoughts wouldn't pour out, and clasping my hands together, I leaned over my knees and stared at the ground.

"You guys, don't I have to die? Isn't that what the Gates of Suffering is supposed to mean, death?" I quietly asked.

"Well, no," Nahum answered. "The Gates of Suffering is supposed to be hell."

"Hell? Oh. Are you saying that, now that I've believed in Jesus Christ, I've been made alive?" Helyn's sparkling eyes gave the answer away before her voice.

"That's it!"

"And since I've been given new life in Christ, I cannot enter hell. Heaven is my new home," I added.

"At last," Nahum exclaimed. Helyn elbowed him. "Ouch! Okay, okay." I laughed.

"She's got you well under control," I teased.

"Not anymore than she's got you," Nahum shot back. Helyn narrowed her eyes and looked between us.

"And don't you forget it," she demanded.

+ + + + + + +

The next day, I met with Robert in the Center. He was seated on the ground, ready to give a lesson in the Scriptures. I seated myself in front of him as I knew I was supposed to.

"Hello, Adrian." Robert looked up from his Bible.

"Hey. What are you reading?" I tried to glance at the passage of Scripture. Robert willingly turned the Bible around and showed me.

"First Corinthians. I heard from Naric that he shared a certain passage with you from here."

"He did?" I asked, clueless. Robert chuckled.

"Yes, he did. First Corinthians 15, verse 55," he prompted. I scanned the verse he pointed out and then nodded.

"Oh, yeah. 'Where, O death, is your victory? Where, O death, is your sting?'" I quoted.

"Do you understand this?" Robert wondered.

I pondered my answer, thinking back to what Helyn had said last night.

"I'm beginning to," I said slowly. Robert smiled.

"What have you begun to understand?" he questioned.

"I've only grasped at the concept of hope in our grief. Helyn and I were talking last night, and she shared that Christians have hope because, one day, all Christians will meet in heaven."

"Yes, that is this verse's deeper meaning," Robert said. "Let me read the passage in context and show you. 'Listen, I tell you a mystery: We will not all sleep, but we will all be changed – in a flash, in the twinkling of an eye, at the last trumpet. For the trumpet will sound, the dead will be raised imperishable, and we will be changed.' And going down to verse 54, 'When the perishable has been clothed with the imperishable, and the mortal with immortality, then the saying that is written will come true: Death has been swallowed up in victory. Where, O death, is thy victory? Where, O death, is thy sting?'"

"I don't get it," I mentioned.

"Here, Paul writes of the coming of our Lord. When Jesus Christ returns to gather His children, and we go to live with Him in heaven, eternally. In heaven, everything is perfect. No more tears, no more pain, no more sin. No more death."

"I like the sound of that," I asserted. Robert nodded.

"Indeed. Are you ready for some sword-play, young man?" he asked. I jumped to my feet, wobbled slightly, and then gave him a battle stance.

"Put a sword in my hand and let me at that sack!"

# CHAPTER THIRTEEN

## The Fighter Inside

"Adrian, get up!" Nahum said, urgently. I opened my eyes and slowly sat up, trying to wake myself.

"Get your things and get out of the tent," Nahum said, shaking my shoulders. I groggily grabbed my few things and got out. Nahum immediately began to collapse the tent.

"What are you doing?" I asked him, shaking my head to wake myself up more.

"We're moving," Nahum said.

"Phantom Warriors?" Nahum nodded. Now, I was fully awake.

"Our scouts have reported their advancement. A number greater than we could count. Naric ordered us moved to the Fort."

"The women and children are already at the Fort. I thought we were staying here to fight," I puzzled.

"Not with that number coming," Nahum shook his head. "We'll need all the protection we can get."

"Wait, we're supposed to be breaking off to defeat Death," I pointed out. Nahum turned to me.

"Commander Naric ordered everyone, you included, to the Fort. When he's ready for us to go down there, he'll say something. Get to the horses."

I opened my mouth to argue with him, but thought better of it and limped quickly to find a horse. Naric was there, urging everyone onto horses, not letting them stop to take down tents or grab their things. This was a side of the Defenders I had never seen. Clearly, the war about to come would be devastating.

"Adrian, get on!" Carissa rode up alongside me. I took her hand and swung up behind her. Carissa tilted her head to look at me.

"You're not steering this time?" she asked.

"Nah, I want to see you do things your way," I replied.

"Too bad. I was looking forward to another high-speed bareback ride," Carissa said, grinning and playfully jabbed my ribs with her elbow.

"Get going! If we survive this war, I'll give you another high-speed bareback ride," I promised. Carissa laughed and kicked the horse's barrel.

Our trip to the Fort was uneventful, though far from silent. Each horse was carrying two people, older men and inexperienced young men like me. Several women and girls, like Carissa and Helyn, were also riding. They had not yet been evacuated for different reasons. Hundreds of armed men ran alongside and behind our group of riders, alert and focused. The ride seemed to last forever. I glanced back at The Enclave when we eventually left it behind. Less than half of the tents were collapsed, yet the place appeared deserted.

Only a solid two hundred men or so were staying put for the next hour or more to guard our rear.

At last, our large group arrived at the Fort. We poured in the gates, filling the place quickly. Women and children ran to meet their husbands and fathers, only to be warned and sent running for safety in underground cellars and the rooms in the stone walls. The men, not waiting to catch their breath, rushed up the towers and ladders to the walls. Many set up the cannons, loading, and aiming them. Several groups grabbed supplies of arrows and positioned themselves as told. I saw Colin take control of the foot soldiers. Carissa pulled our horse to a stop, and I slid off, landing on my good leg.

"We have a few minutes, you should come eat," Carissa said. "It's the women's duty to provide the troops with nourishment. Hopefully, our runner-up unit will come before the Phantom Warriors begin the fight."

"You want me to eat?" I questioned. Carissa flashed a smile.

"Absolutely. You didn't get breakfast. Leave the horse and come with me," she instructed. Through the maze of Defenders, Carissa led me to one of the many kitchens the Fort had. The room was about the size of the Center, and blistering heat consumed the place. Women busily worked in the space, preparing food for the men. The number of people in the building made it feel small. Carissa led me to a table and got me a plate of food and jug of water.

"When you've finished eating, report to Naric. He's in charge of your duties," Carissa said. "I have to go feed some more of the troops." I ate the small meal quickly, and then hurried back outside. The liveliness and purpose continued, despite the meal everyone was eating. Naric was talking to a group of Defenders when I found him, but just as I might have gotten his attention, the runner-up Defenders were spotted. Naric ran by, and I grabbed his arm.

"Naric, what do I do?" I asked. Naric didn't look directly at me.

"Just get up on the wall with Nahum and wait. This isn't your part of the fight."

"Shouldn't I...?"

"Not until the Phantom Warriors are truly distracted, Adrian. Now get on the wall," he commanded. I slunk up the wall. Nahum, his detachment of Defenders, and perhaps three hundred more Defenders stood on this section of the wall. Most had bows and quivers of arrows, while several groups manned the fifteen cannons.

"This is the part I dread," Nahum mentioned. "The waiting is enough to kill you."

"Sure," another Defender agreed. "But at least we have time to prepare to die." I grimaced. The next few minutes of waiting, however, did not prepare me to die. When the Phantom Warriors broke into the open,

I watched them come closer with rising determination not to die.

Then, cannons went off, arrows were shot, men shouted, and Phantom Warriors got close enough to hurl weapons at the top of the wall. I waited tensely for Naric's order, crouching behind a battlement, and holding my sword close to my side. Suddenly, the wall shook, and we all held on to keep from falling.

"What was that?" I asked, turning to Nahum. He shook his head. When he looked over the wall, his face got pale.

"Death's men are firing something at the walls," Nahum started. Again, the walls shook and started to crumble. "And this place isn't going to stand much longer," he finished. "Everyone, get off the wall!" Nahum shouted, grabbing my arm to make sure I obeyed. We jumped from the wall and landed on the ground. My lame leg shouted a warning, which I chose to ignore. We looked back. The wall still held for the moment. Men from the wall rushed back to open the doors and pull the women and children from that section. After another two minutes of trembling, the wall gave way, exposing the Defense. I knew some women and children hadn't gotten out. The Phantom Warriors began to pour into the Fort.

"Adrian!" Naric's voice rose above the clamor. He was running toward us, sword drawn, with hundreds of Defenders behind him. "Now!" I nodded vigorously.

"Nahum, come on!"

The battle scene I ran away from became a horrible mess quickly. Defenders and Phantom Warriors fought and fell so fast I couldn't discern the details. Nahum ran at my side. We dashed for the other side of the Fort, where Alex climbed down to meet us.

"Where have you been?" I shouted at him.

"Got left behind with the runner-up unit!" he answered.

"Adrian, we can get through the gate, but we'll have to make ourselves a path," Nahum cried over the roar of battle. Helyn suddenly appeared, bow and arrows in hand. My team was complete. We charged into the fray. Nahum went first, clearing most of the Phantom Warriors. Alex and I picked off anyone who got past him, and Helyn snuck along behind us. We cleared the gate and found a couple of horses, frightened from the battle, prancing around in the field. Nahum and Helyn snagged the reins.

"Hurry up!" Nahum shouted as he offered me a hand up. We rode double and galloped to the Underground entrance Carissa and I had gone through just a couple weeks ago. Leaving the horses behind, we ran into the tunnels, taking one after another. We couldn't afford to lose too much time. Every second, another Defender could fall.

I tried not to limp too much and keep a steady pace. Nahum walked evenly with me, watching every shadow. Suddenly, he pointed with his Faze Whip.

"Door," Nahum said. I followed his gaze.

"In secret underground tunnels?" Alex asked disbelievingly. "What's in there? Someone's bedroom?" I peered into the room beyond through the small, crudely cut window. A long line of men sat chained to the floor. Their heads were down, and they moaned as one. Beyond them, straight ahead was another door.

Helyn peered into the place over my shoulder. "How sad," she murmured. I touched the handle and pushed the door open.

"What are you doing?" Alex asked. I ignored him, stepping into the room. None of the men looked up. The slap of dank air that hit me made my stomach churn. I strode across the room to the other door, while footsteps pattered behind me as the others followed. I peered into the next room through the window. The small, closed-in space was only lit by an immense flame the color of Death's eyes that stood like a column and wisped about the room.

My first impulse was to open the door and walk into the room. After a momentary hesitation, I did. The ice-blue wisps of the flame came toward me. My eyes scanned the room beyond and around the flame. Beyond the blue light, shadows and darkness enveloped the space. I turned to stare at the flame again; it pulsed, dimming and brightening by turn. The others had finally followed me into the room, gazing around with an expression of confusion.

"Maybe..." Helyn began, her voice shaking, "... maybe we should go back." Nahum nodded. Before

I could agree or raise a protest, I wasn't sure which I would have done, Death's whisper echoed in the room.

"Let's finish this, Adrian Falkner!" he hissed.

Suddenly, the door to the room slammed shut. Helyn screamed. We all readied our weapons. Then came the eerie silence. We formed a circle with our backs to each other. We were ready to move the second Death appeared. My eyes adjusted to the darkness more with each passing second. Every little shadow began to catch my attention. I frowned and tightened my grip on my sword.

"When is the creep going to show?" Alex asked, his voice low. I shrugged and shook my head. Even though I knew that Death wanted the tension to make me uneasy, the anxiety still had its effect on me.

"Look out!" Nahum shouted. Death came out of nowhere, seeming to form with every step that he stealthily took towards us.

Instantly, Helyn whirled around and fired an arrow at Death. He dodged it and produced a sword. I launched forward, and the steel of our blades met. Nahum and Alex quickly followed, striking out at the same time. Death pushed me backwards and ducked beneath the other blows. Nahum's and Alex's blades whizzed through the air.

Death took two steps back. Nahum jumped and landed behind him, slashing out with the Faze Whip. Death ducked, then ran toward me. I brought my sword down to meet him, but Death suddenly disappeared. I swung around, and my blade was within inches of hitting him as he reappeared. He blocked Alex's attempt quickly and pushed him away as I ran closer. Death deflected my blade and then put me on the defense. His strokes were so quick and clean that I parried his first round of intended blows by pure instinct. Death's sword became simply a quick flash of light. It pounded my sword over and over. Then, I lost my grip, and my sword dropped harmlessly to the ground a foot away. Death swung again. I ducked, and then his leg came and bowled me over.

"I should have gotten rid of you when I had the chance," Death growled.

"You can't," I claimed defiantly. I reached for my sword, but Death kicked it out of my reach.

"Will you never finish what you were intended to do?" Death snapped.

"We'll finish it right now," Nahum said, preparing to swing his Faze Whip. Death spun around, striking Nahum on the head and sending him flying a few feet where he landed limply. I grimaced.

"Save your sister," Death insisted, hurriedly getting to the point. I looked to where he was pointing at my sister, who appeared out of nowhere. Miriam's eyes were full of expectation. My eyes went back to Death.

"You don't want me to save her. Why don't you come out and say what you mean? You want my soul and Miriam is nothing but a mirage!" I challenged.

"So, now you're playing clever with me?" Death taunted.

"And you're still avoiding the truth," I accused, rising to my feet. Watching Death's face carefully, I took a battle stance. I needed a powerful weapon, and I was pretty sure I knew where to get it.

"Truth can be so fluctuating. What you think you know is not always so," Death said.

"The same goes for you," I retorted.

"That is because you do not know what truth is."

"I know One who is truth: Jesus Christ!" I shouted. Instantly, Miriam's mirage vanished. Death surged toward me, but I stood unflinchingly. "I'll answer now. Jesus Christ saves." Death halted mid-step and blinked. Behind him, Alex inched towards my sword, and Helyn pulled back her bowstring with an arrow nocked. "Just as I thought, You fear Him," I continued. "Because you know Jesus holds the keys to death and hell."

"Adrian!" Alex grabbed my sword and tossed it. Helyn released her arrow and Death reeled from the unexpected blow. I snatched the sword from the air and turned to face the foe. Alex joined me. Then, we rushed toward him, brandishing our weapons.

Death blocked Alex's blow with his weapon, and mine with an arm. He shoved Alex back a step and swung for my head. I leaned back and swiped my blade at his. Death kicked Alex's right hand, then lunged for me. I leapt back, then forward again, bringing my sword down from over my head. Alex circled around to strike from behind. Death swung with great force, slamming my sword brutally, and I lost my grip. Death whirled around and deflected Alex's weak blow. Then, he drove his sword right into Alex's legs. Helyn fired another arrow, and I dropped to the ground to avoid it. This time, Death was unaffected by the arrow's flight straight through his body. He came straight for me. I jumped back to my feet, but Death's arm met me, striking across my face and sending me back to the ground.

"Give up!" Death commanded, in his now all-too-familiar whisper.

"My soul belongs to my Lord, Jesus Christ," I declared. "I will not give up." Death lifted me above the ground, and then threw me. I flew through the air for a second. Then, I was falling; falling beneath the ground, hurtling down at break-neck speed. I didn't even have time to scream before slamming on the bottom.

My right shoulder hammered with pain and a tight, tingly sensation went up and down my arm. My vision blurred momentarily and I blinked rapidly to clear it. Slowly, I raised myself from my stomach, breathing heavily. Glancing up, I saw the opening of a chasm. Blue light pulsed above me, giving the chasm's entrance a clear outline. The sheer, rock wall was dim. A few projections darkened the wall in a jagged pattern.

"Jesus, help!" Helyn's voice shrieked. Shakily, I stood to my feet, clenching my jaw. I leapt up, grabbing the nearest projecting rock, and began climbing up.

With Helyn's shouts and shrieks ringing in my ears, the climb seemed agonizingly slow. At last, I reached the top with both hands and pulled myself back to ground level. As I rolled away from the edge and picked myself, I saw my sword lying a few feet away. I quickly limped to get it. I picked it up and then locked my eyes on Death. The blue flame separated us. Helyn stood a foot or so away, cowering from him, but neither were armed.

"Leave her alone!" I shouted. Death's eyes found me and widened slightly in surprise, adding piercing beams to the light in the room. I tried not to flinch.

"So, you will protect her? This little temptress? Have you become so blinded you cannot see through her pitiful lies?" Death confronted. "The Defenders are using her to set you up."

"It is you who used a girl to set me up," I shot back.

"And the Defense couldn't have sunk so low as to use the same method, could they? They are not honorable, Adrian Falkner! They've lied to you from the start and are only using you to get rid of me."

My eyes sought Helyn's. There had never been such a pleading look in them. She wanted me to fight Death.

"Not really a bad thing, is it?" I asked, shifting my weight uneasily.

"Listen!" Death hissed. "There is no God, no redemption from sins, no salvation for your soul. The Scriptures don't say that." Death had a point. I had never seen the Scripture for myself. What if it was just his interpretation?

"Yes, they do!" Helyn dared to shout. "Romans 10:9!" Death produced a knife from nowhere and leapt on Helyn.

"That'll be enough!" Death spat. Helyn's wide, brown eyes stared through the blue flame at me. I stared back, unable to move.

"It's over, Adrian Falkner," Death taunted. "Say goodbye to this temptress, you can do nothing to stop me. You're dead!" His voice nearly changed from a whisper. Death raised his weapon to strike, but I had an answer. My voice started soft and hoarse, but slowly, as each word came out, my voice rose until the last word was a shout.

"I was dead, but now, in Christ, I have been made alive!" With that last word ringing in the air, I surged forward and struck the rock between us. It shattered, and the pulsing blue light flashed out as the debris shot across the room. Ignoring the stinging debris, which felt like a million nettles against my skin, I leapt in front of Death and lunged. He shrank back, avoiding the tip of my sword, and freed Helyn.

Without a second's hesitation, I thrust my blade at him repeatedly, forcing Death to back up. If it hadn't been for his ice-blue eyes, I would never have kept track of him in the dark that pervaded the room. Steadily, those eyes pulsed and stared me down, but there was no grip of terror for them to hold over me. Death's dark shape shifted, and it seemed that he had raised his arms in his typical defense pose.

"Jesus Christ has set me free from sin…and death!" I shouted, swinging my blade down with all my might.

There was but a hint of resistance. A whispery shriek told me Death was wounded. A wound in exchange for Alex's. I spun around and aimed my strike at the enemy's face. He staggered back and the light in his eyes dimmed significantly. The dark caused me to hesitate. With a gentle, growing flickering stream, light began to fill the small room from behind me. Death's crippled form shrank from me just a foot away. I took a step closer.

"You can't defeat me," Death said, gasping and choking. My hands clenched the sword's hilt firmly.

"I don't have to. Jesus Christ already did. Consider this good measure," I replied, thrusting my sword straight through his body. Noiselessly, his form lurched and then faded from sight. At last, the deed was done.

# CHAPTER FOURTEEN

## My Soul Made Ready

I whirled around and found Helyn standing with a lantern in her uplifted hand. The beam made her face glow and sparks of fire seemed to dance in her brown eyes. She smiled.

"Great light," I commented lamely.

"We can talk about it later," Helyn said, waving her hand in the air. "How is your arm? You seem to favoring it."

"It'll be fine. Alex and Nahum?"

"I was just about to check. I didn't want you to lose the light because I moved," Helyn explained, rushing across the room. Even with the ruddy lantern-light, Alex's face was pale. The gash on his leg had quickly bled through his pants.

"Check on Nahum," Helyn instructed me, tearing Alex's pant leg so she could get a better look at the wound. As I stepped away, Helyn teasingly addressed Alex. "Wow, soldier. Have a run in with a raccoon?"

"Not quite," Alex grimaced. "It was a raccoon wielding a sword." For some reason, I couldn't help chuckling along with Helyn. At least Alex seemed okay. Nahum was right where he'd collapsed, his Faze Whip just inches from his limp hand.

"He's still unconscious," I called out. Nahum moaned.

"No, I'm fine," he muttered. "My head hurts like crazy, and all my muscles ache, but help me up, Adrian."

"What did he say?" Helyn asked. I frowned.

"I don't know. I think he's still out of it."

"Am not," Nahum growled, struggling to sit up. Dropping my sword, I decided to help him to the desired position.

"Wonderful, he's good," Helyn beamed from across the room. I shot her an incredulous look. Was she teasing?

"Yes, I am," Nahum agreed, grabbing his Faze Whip.

"Take your time. Death is gone, so we're in no hurry," I told him.

"What about the other Defenders at the Fort?" Nahum posed, looking me straight in the eyes.

"The Phantom Warriors are probably gone," Alex asserted, also sitting up.

"What makes you say that?" Helyn wondered.

"Well, our enemy was a ghost, so we might as well assume all his buddies were too, right? So, when their leader dies, there go the troops," Alex said. Nahum shakily rose to his feet and I offered him a hand. He didn't take it.

"I don't think that's the way things work," Nahum protested.

"There's only one way to find out," Helyn announced, jumping up with the lantern in one hand and reaching down her other hand to give Alex a lift. "Let's go back to the Fort."

"All right, fine. Let's go," Alex agreed. Helyn offered her support to Alex, since Nahum and I were so shaken ourselves.

"By the way," Nahum said, bumping my shoulder with the blunt side of his Faze Whip, "Commander Naric's going to want a report."

"Here's my report," I replied, sliding my foot along my sword's blade quickly and grasping the handle as it lifted toward me. "Where, O death, is your victory? Where, O death, is your sting?"

We walked back into the antechamber, and I steeled myself for the sight of men chained to the walls. Instead, a very different sight greeted us. Every chain was broken, and a single man stood in the room, raising his hands and crying out "Praise God!"

"How odd. Do you think we should ask him to go with us?" Helyn wondered. Suddenly, the freed man began to disappear, as if he was fading into the ground. In a matter of seconds, he was gone.

"What is going on?" Nahum murmured.

"I'm telling you, it's all about the enemy. Ghost Death is gone, and all his prisoners were set free," Alex said.

"And how do you explain the prisoners disappearing?" Helyn posed.

"Maybe they were never really here to begin with," Alex said. I sighed.

Although, I wasn't sure what was happening, the effect it had could not be ignored. I felt free. It was like I, too, should have raised my voice to praise God that I was released form chains.

"Look, Alex, I don't know about your theory, but let's get back and prove it. Whether you're right or wrong, I know I'll never hear the end of ghosts until we figure it out," I said. Nahum shoved me from behind.

"Well, hurry up!"

+ + + + + + +

Alex was proven correct, oddly enough. It seemed that, at the exact moment of Death's demise, all of the Phantom Warriors had vanished. This left the Defenders to care for the wounded, bury their dead, and move back into The Enclave. It was a week-long process. We had been settled but a day in The Enclave when Titus declared a prayer service for the families and friends of lost loved ones. Nearly everyone went. Those who were too wounded to come, I learned, were later visited by Titus himself. Nahum was strictly on bed-rest with a concussion, so I struck out alone and joined Helyn and Alex among the crowd. Titus spoke calmly, confidently, even cheerily, to the large crowd that had gathered. I looked around at the faces of Defenders, searching for the familiar peace.

It was there. Amongst all the faces, there was not one, even among the children, without the undetectable aura of peace and hope in Jesus Christ. Finally, my gaze fell on Helyn. She was kneeling in the sand with her eyes closed, mouthing the words of her prayer.

Sensing my gaze, Helyn looked up. "You okay?" she asked.

I glanced around one last time and nodded slowly. "Yeah. I think so. I'm just…you know, I can't help but wonder if the quest was worth their sacrifice."

"Undoubtedly," Helyn smiled. "The quest to save just one soul is worth thousands of Christians' lives. Just ask them." She gestured to the people around us. "They were called into this quest just as much as you were. Called to fight by your side, support you through everything, and give their lives if needed to save your soul. Jesus Christ gave them that calling and it is to His side that these fallen have gone. Nothing has been lost in the kingdom in heaven."

"What does that mean?" Alex inquired, teetering as he walked closer. Alex's wound was healing great, but he still favored his leg in Helyn's presence.

"It means that these people are in heaven," I answered him. "And, now, if I die, I will also join them at Jesus' side."

"So, you're getting involved in the war for souls?" Alex posed melodramatically.

"That's a good way to see it, Alex," Helyn praised. I swallowed a laugh at Alex's almost shocked expression.

I knew he wasn't being serious. Helyn probably did, too.

"Well, I told you," Alex said, pointing a finger at my chest, "that you'd get involved in a war."

"I haven't given up Ledo," I protested.

"Yet," Alex pushed. Shaking my head, I wondered how none of the Gospel message had hit Alex like it had me. I decided to ask him about it later, when Helyn wasn't around.

"Where's Naric?" I asked instead. Helyn glanced around and gave a shrug.

"Try the Tent of Meetings. He may be alone," she suggested. I left the gathering behind and wove through the newly erected tents. The Enclave had begun to take on a distinguishable pattern to me, so I knew where I was headed. I had to slow down to pass through the 'kitchen' which was currently under reconstruction.

"Wait!" an unfamiliar voice abruptly called. I turned and found a young man, probably a couple years older than me, running to catch up. "You're Adrian Falkner, right?" he asked.

"Yeah."

"I just had to catch you," the young man said.

"Why?" I couldn't help the ridiculous question.

With a quick motion, he swiped the hair out of his eyes and said, "because you're the one who defeated Death. I wanted to thank you."

"Oh. Well, you don't have to..." I began. The young man shook his head.

"You don't understand. Hush! My dad died in the last battle two years ago. He was one of many, but..." his eyes filled with tears and he left the thought to be finished in my mind. He continued, "I've tried to stay close to you while you trained because I wanted to know how you would defeat Death. I thought it was impossible in this life. It was meant to hurt. I begged the story out of Nahum and...well, it's gone."

"I still don't understand," I told him. The young man smiled.

"The pain of losing my dad. I've finally replaced my pain with the anticipation of seeing him in heaven one day. This week has been the most peaceful in all my life. And it's because I heard how you changed and overcame Death. So, thanks."

"Uh, you're welcome," I stammered. I couldn't believe who was standing in front of me. It was the same image of the man who had remained in the Underground prison!

"I'll let you go now," the young man said, turning to leave.

"Hey, what's your name?" I asked.

"Connor Balfour. I'm of Colin's kinship."

"So, I'll see you around, I guess," was my reply. Connor nodded and then left. *That was cool*, I thought. With a sense of satisfaction, I took off for the Tent of Meetings again and found the place effortlessly. I paused outside the tent, leaning down to massage my injured leg, then brushed the flap back and looked in. Six of the Seven Leaders were present. Only two of them felt like strangers to me. They all stood in a circle, talking in low tones. Naric turned and motioned me in. I felt like I was intruding, but yielded to his insistent call.

"We were just discussing you," he said.

"Me? When the service is going on out there, you are in here discussing me?" I asked.

"It seemed an appropriate time to talk over the completion of your quest. Give the people a reason to celebrate," Colin said, his usual jovialness in his voice.

"You seem a little surprised to hear about the quest," Naric observed.

"I guess I just hadn't let it sink in that it was done," I answered. "With all the moving, healing, and everything...I don't know. It's been a little hectic, I guess."

"I do want to ask," Naric began, "if you will stick around and keep changing, even though the initial quest is finished?"

"Where's the fun in leaving? Of course, I don't want to leave. I'm not sure how much more I can change, but I want to know more about Christ," I said.

"Well, I can continue to train you in the days to come," Colin said heartily.

"Hear, hear!" Robert agreed.

"Let's welcome our newest Defender!" Howard said. The leaders cheered.

"Wait, a Defender? Me?" I queried, in a shocked tone. Naric chuckled.

"That's the entire purpose of the quest; to get you involved so you might become a believer and Defender. That is unless now you're going to refuse," Naric said, eyeing me amusedly.

"No way!"

+ + + + + + +

"I've got a question for you, Adrian Falkner," Helyn said, as we walked through the rows of tents a day later.

"Okay," I replied slowly.

"What are you going to do with Blake Rileder?" she asked. I furrowed my brow and looked at her.

"What do you mean?"

"Oh, come on," Helyn said playfully, giving me a cheery smile. "Everyone knows that he's out to get revenge for you defeating him." I shook my head.

"I'll probably knock him down like I always do. Revenge is something he's been looking for since we met."

"I see," Helyn answered, losing her playful touch. I looked at her thoughtfully.

"What?"

"I've got a confession to make. I saw you fighting Blake on the Ledo field, you know, back when you did that. It's been weeks now. I heard from James that it happens a lot. I guess it's that fiery anger that you have," Helyn said, looking at me amusedly. I raised an eyebrow at her, but she seemed to ignore it. "Maybe you should lay low for a while. I mean, do you know how easy it was to track you? What if Death comes back for revenge? He wouldn't have to look far."

"Yeah, yeah. Death won't be very successful. 'Where, O death, is your victory,' remember?" I said, waving aside her words. "Someone's got to deal with him. Blake, I mean."

"But what good has it done? Has he stopped coming back? Instead, he keeps looking for a way to lure you in," Helyn argued.

"I'm going to lose this fight, aren't I?"

"I'm just saying, give your bad leg and shoulder a break," Helyn smirked.

"I defeated Death with this bad leg and this bad shoulder, can Blake be any worse?"

"You defeated Death?"

"We."

"Okay, seriously, just think about it. Maybe Blake doesn't want to be beaten up any more than you want to rest your leg and shoulder," Helyn quipped.

"If he does?" I posed.

"Don't use a sword," Helyn said.

"Helyn! Adrian!" Carissa swung down beside us. "Naric's looking for you two."

"What for?" Helyn wondered.

"I think he's sending Adrian off to defeat some dark, evil person alone," Carissa said, a mischievous smile playing on her lips. Helyn playfully shoved her friend's shoulders.

"Or," I added, "into the woods to be captured by a spy and chained to a tree."

"Ha, ha!" Carissa faked a laugh. "I had to get Helyn to listen to you somehow."

"Hey!" Helyn objected. I smirked.

"Helyn, I don't plan to use a sword on Blake. I'll just send him to Carissa," I said. Helyn laughed. Carissa flipped her dark-streaked hair.

"Come on, fighter. The Seven Leaders are waiting," she said. We hurried to the Tent of Meetings.

Apart from the leaders, Nahum and Alex were in one corner talking. Another man stood the opposite corner, the same man who had been there several other times. Would I finally get an introduction? He seemed too young to be taking over for a leader and too old to be one of their sons. Alex invited Helyn to join his and Nahum's conversation. She did. Carissa tapped Naric's shoulder to get his undivided attention. The Seven Leaders turned.

"Has Carissa already told you why you're here, Adrian?" Naric wondered.

"Yeah," I smirked. "You're sending me off to fight a dark, evil person alone." Colin laughed.

"Not exactly," Naric smiled. "Now that your quest is complete, it is best for you to return home."

Alex joined me. "We're going home?" he inquired.

"I can't stay here anymore?" I asked.

"You two must be like Helyn," Naric explained. "You have lives inside of Copper Ridge and parents who need to know you're all right. We would welcome your visits."

"And eagerly start training," Colin added. I smiled.

"You can shoot at me next time," I promised him. He nodded.

"So long, for now, Adrian Falkner."

"Take care of that bad leg," Howard directed. "It'll heal over time."

"Sure. Thanks," I said, glancing at Helyn.

"I can't believe we actually defeated a ghost-figure," Alex exclaimed with a grin. "It's was pretty awesome." He turned to Nahum and Helyn. "Of course, you guys will probably forget Adrian and I ever came."

"Not a chance," Helyn claimed. I stepped closer to Titus.

"Carissa was right. Your teaching is great," I said. Titus smiled.

"I'm glad the words of our Savior and His apostles could help you, young Adrian." Nahum came to my side and faked a punch at my good shoulder.

"I give you two weeks," he said. "Then, Faze Whip lesson?"

"Absolutely!"

+++++++

Despite a few additions, my satchel was still too large. Nevertheless, I packed my things into it. I tossed the clothes to the bottom. Then, the Bible Naric had just given me was placed inside. I picked up Fighter from Ancient Days with a smile, the book that had started it all.

"You ready?" Alex asked, stepping inside the tent.

"Nearly. Remember this?" I asked, lifting the book for him to see. Alex grinned.

"I've never been glad to read a history book before," he answered. I laughed.

"Me neither." The book fell open, and I caught sight of the handwritten note in the back.

"Hey, you never read me that one," Alex mentioned, stepping closer. "Does it make sense?" I glanced over the words and nodded.

"Yeah."

"What does it say?"

"'Called into battle by some great light;
Called into belief by your own past;
Called into victory by defeat.'"

"Um..." Alex crossed his arms and frowned at me. "How does that make sense? Wait. I don't want to hear the translation. Last time you explained that book, things began to happen. Explain it to me in a few months." Alex turned and left the tent. As I put the book away, I muttered the explanation to myself.

"I was called into battle by God. I was called into belief by my past because it showed me my need for

Jesus. I was called into victory over death by letting myself be defeated." I wasn't sure whether that was a prophecy fulfilled before my time, but it seemed like it was fulfilled through me.

I stood to my feet and slung the satchel over my good shoulder. I glanced around Nahum's tent, reaching up to grab the cross which hung around my neck again. Colin had gifted me some leather, and Robert had drilled a hole in the top of the cross. The Defenders had done so much to prepare for me to leave. Now, I was ready to go home.

+ + + + + + +

The streets of Copper Ridge looked almost strange as we walked down them once more. It was like coming back from an adventure in a different land. Alex was quiet as we walked. He wasn't limping anymore, I noticed, but then, neither was I and the bad leg still hurt sometimes. So, I didn't say anything about it. Coming to where we took our own paths, Alex turned to look at me.

"I don't know how I'm going to explain this to my parents," Alex started.

"Your parents? What do you think *my* parents are going to say?" I retorted.

"Okay, so I have it easy. Seriously, how do I explain what I've been doing? 'Hi, Mom and Dad. Where have I been? Just battling a ghost figure alongside Adrian and a group of fighters known as the Defense. Oh, and I'm not allowed to tell you where The Enclave is'." Alex animated the fake conversation he was having, waving his hands in the air.

"Sounds good to me," I grinned. Alex smirked.

"I'll use it then."

"Be sure to tell me how that goes," I told him. Alex promised. We went our separate ways.

The road down to my house was empty; I could walk in quiet. My feelings were all mixed up. Was I happy to get back home and be able to explain things to my parents, or did I dread it? I think it was some of both. Instead of trying to plan what to say, like Alex, I tried hard not to think about what to say. Preplanned speeches never went well for me. Abruptly, in a blur of motion, a fist swung toward me and landed square on my jaw.

*Smack!*

I stumbled to the ground and looked up to see who had hit my protesting jaw.

"Blake!" It was clearly him, from the golden mop of hair to the old shoes. He grinned and clenched his fists.

"I told you I'd get revenge," Blake said. "You've been too cowardly to show your face recently, but now that I've finally caught you…get up and fight!" I squinted up at him.

"Alright, you got me. I give, okay?"

"Yeah, right. I see what you're doing. Fight me, Falkner!" I clenched my fists. I wanted to take him so bad. Blake had no idea how easy his defeat would be when compared to Death's. Then, I remembered my talk with Helyn. Laying low would probably make telling my parents everything easier. Against every urge in my body, I stayed on the ground for another moment and then slowly rose. I glared at Blake, but simply I walked past him.

"Get back here, you coward! Oh, come on, Falkner, you know you want to hit me. You want to fight as much as I do," Blake taunted.

"Save it, Blake. And be on the lookout for a spy," I called over my shoulder.

"I will get my revenge, Falkner!" Blake shouted after me. I left him behind, standing in confusion. I was glad he decided not to give chase. I walked the length of the road and came to my house. Taking another deep breath, I climbed up to the porch and opened the door. I winced as I slammed it fully closed. Then, I turned around and found myself facing my parents. Dad must have gotten back from the business trip. He was glaring at me, so I returned the look. Suddenly, I remembered what Nahum had said back when we had been Faze Whip training for the first time: *don't fool yourself, he loves you.* I bit my bottom lip and looked away from him.

"Hi, Mom…and Dad," I said cautiously.

"Oh, Adrian, how good of you to come home," Mom said. She gave me a slow smile, cocked her head, and raised an eyebrow. "Where have you been?"

I looked between her and Dad, who raised both his eyebrows, a sign that he expected the question to be answered.

"Oh, joy," I muttered sarcastically.

Where, O death, is thy victory? Where, O death, thy sting? (1 Corinthians 15:55)

# From the Authoress:

Dear Reader,

The battle in this story represents a spiritual battle that we all face today. Adrian Falkner is confronted by the all-time enemy: Death. As a result of the Fall of Man, death is rampant in our Fallen Land.

As an unbeliever, Adrian is tremendously hurt by the death of his little sister, Miriam. It's unfair. However, as a Christian, Adrian realizes that death was defeated by Jesus Christ when He died on the cross for the sin caused by man and then rose again!

Helyn and the other Defenders give the great reminder of the hope we have for our eternal lives— life everlasting with Jesus Christ, our Savior, and all those who believe in Him.

The book's title, Chained, symbolizes Adrian Falkner's spiritual state. He's chained to his past. When Adrian accepts Jesus Christ's righteousness as his own, and defeats Death through Him, the Messiah breaks Adrian's chains!

Not only Adrian, however, was released. Unbeknownst to Adrian, others were watching him and Conner is an example of those who find freedom in another's victory.

Reader, the world is watching you fight the spiritual battles, and, when you win, you open the path for others to find freedom and hope in Jesus Christ!

May you win the battle over Death, receiving our great hope for the eternal future, and open the way for others to come to our Lord Jesus Christ!

*Alyson Jensen*

# Lexicon

**Adrian Falkner** (a-drEE-in) (fall-ke-ner) – a troubled teen, who is unpredictable, sarcastic, and hurting because of his past. Son of John and Eleanor.

**Alex Zeigler** (al-licks) (zEE-g-ler) – the unlikely and seemingly perfect friend of Adrian, who has a strange fascination with ghosts, yet doesn't love adventure.

**Avric Ocean** (A-v–RICK) (o-SH-en)– the name of the ocean which surrounds much of the Fallen Lands, starting on Chahcan's northern coast.

**Blake Rileder** (blayk) (RILE-der) – a misguided teen who loves to make life miserable for Adrian.

**Bridge's Mansion** (brijiz) (man(t)SH(e)n) – an institute of learning for boys, ages 12 to 19, run by an upper class man called "Bridge."

**Carissa Harris** (CUH-riss-uh) (HAIR-iss) – a spy for the Defense, a friend of Helyn's, who delights in being secretive.

**Chahcan** (kAW-kin) – the Crown of the Fallen Lands, the mainland of Chahcan territory.

**(The) Center** (sen(t)er) – the place where Defenders equip themselves to fight with weapons and the Sword of the Spirit; the Scriptures.

**Colin Burlance** (CALL-in) (bUR-lANce)– a jovial man among the Seven Leaders who teaches Adrian agility.

**Connor Balfour** (kAh-ner) (bAL-fEWer) - a young man of Colin's kinship whose life is changed by watching Adrian fight death.

**(The) Contra** (kONntrUH) – a group comprised of more powerful Phantom Warriors (i.e. Death) who rarely appear and attack at the same time. The term can also refer to their lesser demon armies (see *Phantom Warriors*). The name comes from the English word meaning "to contradict."

**Copper Ridge** (käper) (rij) – the "poverty town" in the land of Chahcan, located in the east, where lower class citizens live. Hometown of Adrian Falkner.

**Death** (deTH)– the mortal enemy of every man, and the one that Adrian must face off against.

**Defencio Veritas** (deh-fENs-ee-OH) (ver-i-TAs) – a group of fighting Christians, who were forced to hide in the forests of Chahcan by the Ruling Heads, yet continue to secretly fight enemies who remain unknown to Chahcan citizens. The name comes from the Latin words which means "Defense of Truth."

**Defender(s)** (de'fENd'er) – used to refer to {a person who identifies as being with} those who are a part and involved with the Defencio Veritas.

**Defense** (de'fens) – see *Defencio Veritas*.

**Damascus** (de'maskes) – a blade made by the process of melting iron and steel together in various layers to ensure toughness, yet flexibility.

**Edmund Naric** ('edmend) (n-AIR-ec) – the commander of the Defencio Veritas' militia and one of the Seven Leaders.

**Eleanor Falkner** (elener) (fall-ke-ner) – Adrian's mother, who tries to be a peacemaker, yet is emotionally wrecked from the death and actions of her children.

**(The) Enclave** (en'kläv) – the territory belonging to the Defense within Chahcan, where they are free to be Christ-followers.

**Fallen Lands** ('fôlen) (land) – the lands (i.e. Chahcan and the countries surrounding it) referred to as a whole.

**Faze Whip** (faz) (wip) – a weapon – with joined shafts made of cedar, a leather wrapped handle, and two curved, *Damascus* style blades on either end – which can unlock and extend another three feet.

**(The) Fort** (fôrt)– an abandoned fortress outside of White Field, where the Defense occasionally retreats for safety and fighting.

**Helyn Thicket** (helen) (THikit)– the graceful and cheery daughter of an important trader in and beyond Chahcan territory.

**Iron Cap** (i(e)rn) (kap) – an industrial town, located in the north of Chahcan, where the working class citizens live.

**James** (jamz) – a guy who plays Ledo with Adrian, but isn't truly his friend.

**John Falkner** (jän) (fall-ke-ner) – Adrian's father, with whom Adrian always seems to be in trouble.

**Kinship** (kin, SHip) – a certain number among the Defenders who are cared for primarily by one of the Seven Leaders.

**Kriff** (kr'if) – a mountainous town, located north-west in Chahcan, where Ruling Heads, upper class citizens, lower class citizens, and working class citizens will live in relative peace.

**Ledo** (lay'dOH) – the game of Chahcan, where one team tries to get a ball past another team to the other end of the field to score points. The name comes from the Latin word which means "to smash".

**(The) Market** (märket) – the trading center of Copper Ridge and White Field, primarily for coin.

**Miriam Falkner** (mir-EE-um) (fall-ke-ner) – Adrian's younger sister, who died at the age of seven from an incurable disease.

**Morro Falkner** (môrOH) (fall-ke-ner) – Adrian's elder brother by six years, who encouraged Adrian to smuggle and then abandoned him.

**Nahum** (nAY-hoom) – a spy for the Defense, and a friend of Helyn's, who desires to be Adrian's friend. Nahum weilds a Faze Whip and teaches Adrian how to use one as well.

**Phantom Warriors** (fan(t)um) (wôrEEurs) – members of the Contra and army of Death; physical representation of demon legions.

**Robert** (räbert) – a sword master, among the Seven Leaders, who instructs Adrian on wielding a sword and in the Scriptures.

**Ruling Head(s)** (rooliNG) (hed) – the combined title and insult the lower class give to any rich, influential person in Chahcan.

**Seven Leaders** (seven) (lee-ders) – a number of men who are responsible for and in leadership over certain groups within the Defense.

**Tent of Meetings** (tent ev meediNGs) – the place where the Seven Leaders gather to speak in counsel and make decisions on battle plans.

**Titus** (tid-es) – another of the Seven Leaders, who leads prayer and Scripture meetings in the Defense.

**Tolo** (toh'loh) – the capital of Chahcan; home of the Ruling Heads.

**Tyrrohn(s)** (ti(e)'rOHns) – {a person involved with} a group of people who seek to gain power through violence, theft, and other unlawful and harmful activities. A title derived from the words "tyrant" and "to own".

**Tyrrohn Ally** (ti(e)'rOHns) (ali(e)) – someone who provides shelter, provisions, and/or takes a bribe to work for the Tyrrohns.

**(The) Underground** (UNder, ground) – a series of tunnels carved during the Wars of Old, which includes a room for prisoners of war.

**Vainus** (vAIN-us) – the second twin town, located south-west in Chahcan; a desert.

**Veaus** (vEE-us) – the first twin town, located north-east in Chahcan; a seaport.

**White Field** (wi(e)t) (feeld) – a countryside town in Chahcan, located in the south, where upper class citizen live. Hometown of Helyn Thicket.

Made in the USA
Middletown, DE
26 June 2021

43174268R00144